True Savage 4:
A Criminal Clan

Lock Down Publications and Ca$h
Presents
True Savage 4
A Novel by *Chris Green*

Lock Down Publications
P.O. Box 870494
Mesquite, Tx 75187

Visit our website @
www.lockdownpublications.com

Copyright 2018 by True Savage 4

First Edition June 2018
Printed in the United States of America

This is a work of fiction. Names, characters, places, and incidents either are products of the author's imagination or are used fictitiously. Any similarity to actual events or locales or persons, living or dead, is entirely coincidental.

Lock Down Publications
Like our page on Facebook: Lock Down Publications @
www.facebook.com/lockdownpublications.ldp
Cover design and layout by: **Dynasty Cover Me**
Book interior design by: **Shawn Walker**
Edited by: **Jill Alicea**

Stay Connected with Us!

Text **LOCKDOWN** to 22828 to stay up-to-date with new
releases, sneak peaks, contests and more…
Or **CLICK HERE** to sign up.
Thank you.

Like our page on Facebook:

Lock Down Publications: Facebook

Join Lock Down Publications/The New Era Reading Group

Visit our website @
www.lockdownpublications.com

Follow us on Instagram:

Lock Down Publications: Instagram

Email Us: We want to hear from you!

Submission Guideline.

Submit the first three chapters of your completed manuscript to ldpsubmissions@gmail.com, subject line: Your book's title. The manuscript must be in a .doc file and sent as an attachment. Document should be in Times New Roman, double spaced and in size 12 font. Also, provide your synopsis and full contact information. If sending multiple submissions, they must each be in a separate email.

Have a story but no way to send it electronically? You can still submit to LDP/Ca$h Presents. Send in the first three chapters, written or typed, of your completed manuscript to:

LDP: Submissions Dept
Po Box 870494
Mesquite, Tx 75187

DO NOT send original manuscript. Must be a duplicate.

Provide your synopsis and a cover letter containing your full contact information.

Thanks for considering LDP and Ca$h Presents.

Note to the reader

When we last left of in TRUE SAVAGE 3, the story focused on Ghost and the others. In this installment you will meet the female savages that come from Ghost's tree, and many new colorful characters. Just ride with me on this savage ride that will all your together in the end.

CHRIS GREEN

Prologue

"Nigga, we been riding around for thirty minutes and we still ain't made it there yet?" Jimmie asked as he puffed on his cigarette.

"Patience, nigga! We almost there. The work isn't going anywhere," Slick said, cutting his eyes at him. They pulled inside the abandoned Amazing Grace restaurant on Simpson Road. They both checked their pistols before exiting the car. The hard breeze danced in the air, making Slick zip up his coat. Jimmie led the way as they walked around the corner.

"Man, what the fuck is going on? These niggas ain't even here yet."

Turning around, Slick collided the 45 automatic across his face, shattering the bridge of his nose. The gun flew out of his hand as Jimmie crashed down on one knee.

"Ahh, fuck!" Jimmie yelled, trying to shake the stars from his vision. Placing his hand on the top of this face, he tried to stop the blood from pouring. "Nigga, I'ma fucking kill you! How are you gonna trade on your own brother about some paper?" Jimmie yelled, looking into the barrel of the gun.

"It's money, and you ain't nothing but my daddy's son." Slick smiled before pulling the trigger twice.

CHRIS GREEN

Chapter 1

Sharon sat back as she listened to her husband's voicemail come on for the eighth time. It wasn't like Jimmie not to answer the phone, especially when it was a call from home. Beep!

"I don't know where the fuck you are, Jimmie, but not picking up the phone is what gon' get yo' ass an empty home if you keep fucking with me. Answer the damn phone!" Sharon screamed through the receiver, then hung up.

She couldn't be madder at that moment. Her two overgrown-ass children were running the streets, her husband continued to get into trouble like he wasn't pushing forty, and her spoiled-ass eight-year-old consistently disobeyed her. She strove hard for her family and for her life. She made a way for her kids to live the way they needed, but they only cared for the things that they chose.

"Mommy!" her daughter screamed, busting through the bedroom door.

"Oh God, what is it now, Reeses?" Sharon said, sighing.

"Where is Justin and Phil, Ma? They supposed to take me to the zoo today." Beaming at Sharon with her dark grey eyes, Reeses stood in front of her, waiting for an answer.

Sharon looked down at her with a sly grin. "Uh, excuse me, little girl. I don't know where your brothers are. I've been trying to find them and your father since six o'clock, honey."

"Well, how about you order some pizza? It's nothing to eat inside the refrigerator," Reeses replied in a sarcastic tone.

Sharon leveled her eyes down at her daughter. "Yeah, and how about you go and wait yo' little ass in the bedroom until it gets here, smart ass."

Reeses giggled at her mother's words while she walked off towards her room. Sharon sat back, wondering where her sons could be. Knowing those two, they were probably doing something that would land them inside a grave or a maximum security prison. She decided to recollect herself. Rolling a blunt and fixing a glass of champagne, she picked up the phone and ordered dinner for the family. Pulling the blunt from her ear, she placed it in between her lips and sparked it up. When the smoke touched her insides, her body instantly relaxed. Sharon wasn't a big fan of crack, but lately she had been sneaking a little inside of a joint every now and then.

Jimmie ended up finding out a few months back that she was playing around with it. He threatened to leave if she wouldn't stop. So she decided to clean her act up a little bit and to be more low key with her using. With all the things she was dealing with around the house, she honestly felt whatever she placed inside her lungs was her business. At forty-one years old, Sharon was still a dime piece. Her ass was still fat and intact, and she didn't have any stretch marks climbing up her stomach. Her pussy wasn't loose like shoestrings and she still carried herself around as she supposed to. She knew one thing for sure: loyalty was guaranteed, running through her blood, and she would do whatever necessary to take care of the family. But Jimmie didn't have too many more chances before she packed her shit and left.

Her two sons coming through the front door knocked away her negative aura.

"Nigga, how the fuck you gon' say that's yo' girl and you ain't even smashed yet?" Phil said to his twin.

"First off, I ain't all about smashing. She a real woman. I'd rather kick back and take my time with her. See, you wouldn't know nun 'bout that. You would rush and cook a pack of noodles in one minute when it clearly says three on the pack, retard."

Phil laughed, taking the gallon of Kool-Aid out of the fridge. "Nigga, I'm the best li'l brother you coulda been blessed with. My pussy rate through the roof. I always chase paper, and I don't trust no niggas. You taught me that."

Justin nodded his head to his brother and turned his attention to their mother.

"Yo, Ma. Why are you getting twisted on a Monday night? I thought you had to be up for work in the morning?"

"Hmm! I do, but a bitch might be dead before I can get there. Stressing over y'all sorry asses. Has either one of you heard from your father?"

"Nah! Pop called me earlier today and said he was gonna be out for a second."

"Your sister is rampaging about you guys taking her to the zoo."

Justin instantly covered his face, burying his thumbs inside his temples. "Fuck! I forgot that was today. Where is she?"

Sharon pointed towards the bedrooms with her "good luck" grin on.

Justin knew that his baby sister would be upset. She was very close to him, more so than anyone else, and it always killed him to break any promise. Reeses was a girl you just couldn't deny.

Knocking lightly on her door, he waited for a response. Cracking the door, Justin peeked inside and walked in.

Reeses sat Indian style in front of her forty-inch flat screen TV, watching Animal Planet. Justin walked slowly over to the center of the room and sat directly beside her. She kept her eyes focused on the screen as if he wasn't even there. Looking at her facial expression, he knew she was beyond mad.

"Reeses, I'm so sorry I didn't make it today. I was so busy that - "

"You lied," she replied, cutting him off.

"Don't feel like that, Reese. How about I take you to the zoo tomorrow?"

"I don't wanna go anymore."

Justin sat quiet for a second before he spoke. "Well, how about we go to the skating house with all the fun games you like to play this Friday?"

Turning her head, she looked at him with excitement. "Are you gonna skate with me this time?"

He smiled at his baby sister, looking in her low grey eyes. "Pinky promise," Justin replied, pulling the pack of buttercups out of his front pocket, knowing the candy was her weakness.

She took it out of his hand with a huge grin. "I forgive you."

"Ahhh! That's my muffin!" Justin yelled, grabbing her into a hug. After making sure his number one was okay, he planted a kiss on her forehead and headed for his room across the hall.

Stepping through the threshold of the room, he closed the door and locked it behind him. Opening his closet, he walked in and removed the wooden plate from his wall. Pulling the Lorcin 9mm handgun from his waist, he placed it on the floor and started to dial the code inside the titanium safe. Deactivating the latch, he opened it up, reaching past the stacks of crispy bills and pulling out the perfectly wrapped kilo of cocaine.

"Justin!" Sharon yelled, breaking him out of his movements.

Closing the safe, he quickly placed the plate back in position.

To do the things Justin did for his family, he had to make sacrifices. He had already hustled for over four years without his father knowing.

14

Sharon's stress level went through the roof when she found out Jimmie was cheating. It wasn't until he found out she was lacing her joints that he started to slide around on her. Jimmie was an all-around magnet. There was nothing scarier than a 6'3", 200 pound man with grey eyes. He practically had his way through the streets. Whatever he wanted, he would just take it. He was a natural born hustler. Unfortunately, the twins branched off to another line of business. If Reeses and his mom were straight, then Justin was straight with doing the things he had to do so he could provide.

Walking out of the bedroom, Justin maneuvered to the living room, where his mom rested on the couch.

"Hey, baby," Sharon said, looking up at him.

"Wassup, Ma?"

"I need you to do me a favor." She giggled, feeling the weed kick in.

"Hold up! I know you ain't high?" he questioned, looking in her eyes.

"Oh, here we go. Did your father put you up to this?"

"What are you talking about?"

"Questioning a grown fucking woman, dumb ass. Now I need some money to go and handle some business tomorrow. Are you gonna help me or not?"

"Why didn't you just ask Pop, Mama? I just gave you a thousand dollars six days ago."

"Your fucking daddy is stingy. He can't shit and wipe the crack of his ass without checking his pocket. All he gives a damn about is Reeses, and I didn't ask yo' daddy, nigga. I asked you!"

"Yo, whatever, Ma. I'll give it to you in the morning," Justin mumbled, rubbing his hand in his head.

Before Sharon could reply the doorbell rang, breaking her attention.

"Who in the fuck is ringing the door at ten o'clock at night?" Justin asked.

"Honey, relax. It's probably just the pizza I ordered."

Opening the door, she greeted the man and grabbed the receipt. After paying for the dinner, she shut the door and placed the food on the kitchen table.

"Reeses! Come and eat, baby."

Justin slid past Sharon, grabbing a slice out of the box.

"You better have washed ya hands too, nasty-ass boy," Sharon complained, fixing her daughter a plate.

"I know that ain't no Papa John's I smell in this bitch?" Phil yelled, coming out of his room.

"Yeah, it is. Calm yo' hyperactive ass down and come eat."

The crashing of the front door caused Reeses to drop her plate to the floor.

"FBI! FBI! Put your fucking hands in the air."

"What in the fuck is going on? Why are you motherfuckers bursting into my house?" Sharon screamed, holding her hands high in fear.

The agents ignored her, rushing over and slamming Phil and Justin to the ground.

"Justin and Phillip Rivers, you are both under arrest for armed robbery and trafficking cocaine to an undercover officer."

"Oh, hell no! My boys ain't did a damn thing. This has to be a mistake!"

"Ma'am, the law doesn't make mistakes. That's gonna be up to a judge to decide. These boys are gonna have to appear in court first."

"Where is your evidence, you son of a bitch? This is a misidentification."

Justin's eyes fell on Reeses when the officer lifted him and Phil off the ground. The expression on her face told him that she was about to cry.

"It's okay, muffin. I just have to go handle this with the officers. Ya hear me?" Justin asked with a small smile.

Her lips began to tremble as the tears started to let loose.

"Hey! Skate World on Friday. I promise. Don't cry, little one."

Nodding her head, she stood beside her mother.

"Ma, get us both a lawyer tonight!"

"I got y'all, baby," she replied, looking at them while the officers led them out of the house.

"Reeses, I want you to go and get ready for bed, baby. Mama has to get this mess with your brothers handled right now."

She looked at Sharon, wiping her eyes. Her once happy face was replaced with disappointment while she headed inside her room.

Hours passed as she sat on the phone with lawyer after lawyer. Sharon began to lose her mind. The charges on their case were major felonies and their legal advisors notified her that they couldn't be released until they appeared in court.

"Damn it!" Sharon screamed, feeling the pressure weighing in on her. She knew that Jimmie would be on her ass.

The federal agents had taken their seventeen-year-old twins into custody and he was nowhere to be found. She began to call his cell again, chewing on the tip of her nails. The continual ringing made the stress level rise even harder.

Digging in her bra, she pulled out the sack of dope and fumbled with it. She slid the stem from her pocket and placed two rocks inside of the pipe. Grabbing the lighter, she placed fire on the other end and inhaled. Her chest began to tighten as she grew numb in satisfaction. The stem fell from her hand when she slumped inside the sofa couch.

Reeses stood in the doorway of her bedroom, looking at her mother spaced out. Walking into the living room, she dragged her blanket over and climbed into Sharon's lap.

Feeling her daughter, Sharon grabbed her lightly and started to rock back and forth. Reeses closed her eyes and clutched on to her tightly. The silence of the house made the atmosphere feel weird. Sharon prayed silently in her head. All she wanted was peace and for the bullshit to end.

Chapter 2

The hard knocking at the door snapped Sharon out of her sleep. The knocking started again when she looked at Reeses asleep in her lap. The sun beamed hard through the curtains, giving the presence of another day. Sliding Reeses over, she stood up and headed for the door. Grabbing the knob, she opened it up quickly.

"Slick? What are you doing here?" she asked with a confused face.

Slick was Jimmie's brother. They shared the same father. Nothing but trouble followed him every time he came around.

"Sharon! It's Jimmie," he said with his head facing the ground.

"What about Jimmie?"

"He's dead, Sharon!"

The words that spilled from his lips cut through her chest and she felt as if she had just been stabbed.

"What did you just say?"

Slick looked Sharon in the eye and told her what would change her life forever.

"Jimmie was murdered last night. He was shot in the head during a shootout."

The horrible scream that she released startled Reeses, walking her up. As Sharon collapsed to the floor, she felt the air in her chest leave, making the cries grow louder.

Walking to her mother's side, Reeses wrapped her arms around Sharon's neck.

It was hard because she didn't understand, but she knew that something was wrong.

"It's okay, Mommy. Justin and Phil are gonna come back. I miss them too," she whined, burying her face in Sharon's shoulder.

Sharon continued to cry, looking at her daughter. How do you tell an eight-year-old daddy's girl that her father will never come back?

Reeses looked at Slick staring down at them and frowned. The evil stare that he wore made the hairs on her neck rise. Helping her off the floor, he held on to her shoulder.

"I'm gonna find out who did this, Shar."

Spitting in his face, Sharon slammed a hard right hand across his cheek.

"Get the fuck off my porch!" she screamed like a madwoman.

Clenching his jaws, he wiped the spit from his face. Looking at Reeses, he gave her a slick smile and walked down the steps. Getting to the bottom, he spoke over his left shoulder.

"You be careful now, Sharon."

Slick opened his car door, got in, and pulled off slowly.

***

4 months later
Federal Court of Law

It had been four months since Sharon had lost her husband and children in one night. No woman, wife, or mother could feel the way that she did at that time in her life. She had spent her past few months getting high off heroin. So many things had come to pass in her life and take her under that she started to devote all her time to the new poison that clogged her brain and numbed the pain. Nothing else but the euphoria of the drugs could take her mind off Jimmie and the boys. Her life had completely derailed from living the dream she always wanted. It was down to just her and Reeses by themselves.

Reeses held on to her hand while she stared at both of her brothers in ankle shackles and suits.

"Does the jury have a verdict yet on this case?" Judge Penson asked.

"Yes sir!" the District Attorney replied in a tone that was more excited than professional.

"In that case, will both the defendants rise for the verdict?"

The short white man that rose from the stand clutched onto the paper in his hand before he spoke. "We, the jury, find Philip and Justin Rivers on the count of armed robbery, not guilty."

The courtroom began to gain life and become loud, making the judge order quiet.

"Jury, please finish."

The man shook his head and continued to speak. "We, the jury, find Philip and Justin Rivers on the count of trafficking cocaine to an undercover officer, guilty!"

Justin looked quickly at Philip and back to his lawyer. "I thought you said that this was under control. What happened?" he asked in an aggressive tone.

"Well, ya see, Mr. Rivers, the evidence from the –"

"Fix it, motherfucker! We paid you fifty grand to make this shit disappear. Now you either fix it, or I'll fix you!" Justin spat while the officers placed him and Phil back in handcuffs.

"Right away, Mr. Rivers," the lawyer agreed nervously, remembering an encounter with Jimmie a few years back.

After Jimmie caught a murder case, he paid Mr. Chizek handsomely to make it go away. The second day of the trial, things began to look shaky, so Jimmie had a few people spend the night with his wife and kids until it was all over, a mission that was handled by Slick personally.

The officers began to escort them towards the back to the holding cells. Reeses stared in silence while her brothers walked away and caught Justin's eye.

The half-hearted smile he gave her said it would all be okay, but she knew her brother well. When the doors closed behind them, her heart closed off to the world. Her father, brothers, and happiness were officially stripped from her life. Tragedy lurked in the air as the family slowly left from existence. The light tears she held in the corner of her eyes fell to the floor.

"Come on, let's go home, baby," Sharon mumbled, grabbing ahold of her hand.

***

The ride home from the courthouse was extremely silent. Sharon observed Reeses facing the opposite way, looking out the window. The distraught look showed that her spirit wasn't so warm anymore. It was clear that they weren't going to see Justin or Philip for a while.

Pulling into the driveway, Sharon parked the car. She looked at Slick, who was leaning against his whip in front of them. The light from his pinky ring and watch danced in the sun as he ended his phone call.

"Wassup, Sharon?" he asked as they climbed out of the vehicle.

"Nothing, Slick."

"How did the trial go with Jack and Poker today?" he asked Sharon, looking down into the grey eyes of her daughter.

"They lost," Sharon replied dryly, handing the keys to Reeses so she could head into the house. "Look, Slick, I know I owe you a few dollars from the last set-up you gave me, but I'ma probably need a little credit until I can get y'all mama to go in Jimmie's stash. You think you holding enough to spare me or what?"

Slick smiled, looking at the time on his diamond encrusted Rolex. "Shit, Sharon, I just blessed you the last three times and you still ain't came correct yet," he complained, grabbing on his crotch.

She sighed heavily, listening to the words slide off his tongue as if she wasn't Jimmie's wife. "You really gon' keep making me do that shit, Slick? I told you I'm not comfortable with it."

"Well, you ain't comfortable getting my shit then," he boasted, running his finger across the line of her breasts.

"Can I just catch you on the next round? Reeses is home with me."

"I ain't got time to be playing these weak-ass games with you. Now is you gon' tell her to go in the other room so we can handle our business or not?" he asked with more of a psycho expression.

Sharon watched Reeses staring at her from the crack of the door and gave in as usual.

"Baby, go into your room for a little while so Mama can handle something."

Eyeing Slick, Reeses walked slowly to her room and closed the door.

Entering the master bedroom, Slick pulled the sack of dope from his pocket and tossed it on the bed.

"Serve then splurge, bitch. I get me first," he teased, pulling his dick out.

Holding back her tears, Sharon got on her knees and took a deep breath before taking him into her mouth.

Within the first five minutes, Slick was holding on to her hair and releasing himself inside her throat. "Fuck!" he moaned as she choked and threw up all over his pants and Mauri Gators.

The hard punch that came down across Sharon's face caused Reeses to jump on the other side of the door.

"Bitch! Learn how to hold that shit, hoe. You fucked up my jeans," he yelled when she fell into the corner. Slick stormed out of the room.

Sharon didn't budge until she heard the front door close. She wiped her face and got up, grabbing the package off the bed. Making her way to the dresser, she grabbed the supplies to break the substance down into her syringe. The fumbling of her fingers made it worse as she tried to balance it all on the spoon.

"Mommy?" Reeses said behind Sharon, scaring her.

"Goddammit, girl! What is it?" she yelled, getting agitated from the monkey on her back.

"That stuff always makes you mad when you come out of your room."

Before Sharon could think twice, her back hand slammed into Reeses's cheek, sending her to the ground.

"Don't you ever talk to me like that, bitch! I'm your mama! Now get up and get the fuck out!" she yelled, trying to place the needle by the right vein.

Reeses's eyes never left Sharon's face as the small line of blood dripped from her lips to the floor. At that moment, she knew whatever had her mother in that state of mind at that time would never let her go. Standing up, she wiped her lips and walked out of the room, closing the door behind her. Her heart wanted to understand so badly about her mother's trials and tribulations, but the rage and pain she felt pouring through her veins was a place she knew that she never wanted to be. Her mind knew that her mom was lost behind a door that could never be re-opened.

CHRIS GREEN

Chapter 3

It was two-thirty in the afternoon and Reeses sat on the bus, heading home. The laughter and chaos from the kids was so overbearing the bus driver had to stop in traffic twice.

Reeses's hand moved to her stomach, feeling the growl that rumbled inside. The thought of eating the snacks she had stashed on the shelf at home made her smile as the bus headed towards her street. The sudden stop made her jerk forward in the seat. Homicide cars and ambulances surrounded the perimeter while assistants moved through the crowd quickly.

Approaching the bus, a detective wearing a trench coat knocked sternly on the door. After having a quick conversation with the driver, he walked back to Reeses and escorted her off the bus.

"Reeses!" Tasha screamed, rushing to her side and closing her in a tight hug.

Before she could tell her anything, the stretcher that rolled from the house caught her attention. Her soul almost left her little body when she saw her mother's arm dangle from under the sheet.

Snatching herself away from Tasha, Reeses screamed and ran to her mother's side. The EMS tech clasped ahold of her hand before she could remove the cover.

"Nooo! Let me go!" she cried, snatching the bracelet off Sharon's wrist by accident. "Mommy, get up!"

Tasha grabbed Reeses's arm, pulling her back while the EMS team retreated inside the ambulance and pulled off. The sobs and screams that she released in Tasha's shirt only made it worse. She couldn't really imagine the hurt that Reeses contained inside, but she knew it was her mission to keep her straight.

The lead detective stood behind them with a sad face while they grieved over Sharon.

"Ma'am? Are you willing to take the child into custody? If not, she will have to go with Child Services."

Tasha looked up with tears running down her face.

"I'll take full responsibility for her at all cost. No one is taking her nowhere."

"It's okay. No one is gonna take her away from you. I just need a little paperwork filled out and you are all free to go."

***

It had only been a week since Tasha pulled Reeses into her home. Tasha couldn't help it, but the attitude and depression Reeses was carrying around started to become annoying.

She knew that something had to tighten up. In her head, Reeses wasn't paying any bills nor was she heading out to the strip club every night to shake her ass. Tasha really was never into the watching kids thing. Sharon was only her stepsister, but she was the only sibling left who could take Reeses besides Jimmie's stepmom. But she was living in a nursing home ever since his death and his sister was supposedly under investigation by the law, so there was no other option but for Tasha to take her in.

The doorbell ringing broke Tasha out of her small trance. She was already thirty minutes late for work and hadn't introduced Reeses to her babysitter yet.

"Little girl, you need to come out here. It's time for me to get to work," Tasha yelled, gathering her things.

Tasha opened the door, revealing a 5'8" tall man with an athletic build. He sported an all-white Falcon snap back and a white T-shirt. His eyes were dark, and his facial expression spelled a true gangsta.

"Come on in, boy," Tasha said with a huge grin on her face.

Reeses stood in the middle of the room, eyeing the man standing in front of her.

"Reeses, this is your babysitter, Ghost."

"What type of name is that?" Reeses replied, looking confused.

"It's okay, li'l mama. It's just my childhood name my friends called me. Your name is Reeses, like the candy, right?"

A smile spread across her face when he pulled the pack of candy from his jacket. "Thank you!" Taking the candy, she sat in front of the television.

"She should be just fine," Ghost said, smiling.

"Thank you, Ghost. Two hours tops!"

"Listen. Is there any way you can let me take her back to Tiffany? She's really the last thing missing to close this chapter of Jimmie."

"Look, Ghost, no disrespect, but I have her in my custody. Tiffany has never been around for her before. I feel that I need to do this for Sharon. If it comes out to be different, I will let you all know."

Ghost nodded his head as she headed out of the door.

"How did you know I like Reese's cups?" Reeses asked when he sat on the couch.

"Because you've been eating them since you were two."

"Well, how come I can't remember you?"

"Me and your dad used to work together. He was my friend and I married his sister, your Auntie Tiffany."

Reeses sat quietly while she pondered Ghost's words.

"So, you're my uncle?"

"Yes, little mama. I'm your uncle."

The rest of the night ran smoothly. She told Ghost all the stories of her mom and dad and even a little about her brothers, whom she missed.

As time swept by, Tasha came moving through the door with a bottle of champagne in her hand.

"Hey y'all. How did everything go?"

"Auntie Tasha? Does he really have to go now? We just started having fun."

Ghost chuckled lightly and picked her up. "It's okay, little one. I'll be back to see you!"

Her smile brightened and she held out her pinky. "Do you promise?"

Grabbing her pinky, he looked into her grey eyes. "I promised your daddy I wouldn't let anything happen to you. I promise I'm not gonna leave ya. I'll be here if you need me."

"Bye, Uncle Ghost," she whispered, hugging his neck tight.

Everything seemed like it was crashing down for her, but Ghost wasn't the average uncle. He was special, an uncle who would protect family at any cost.

After he left, Tasha sat and spoke to Reeses, not as an auntie, but as a sinner. This would be the talk that sent a good girl down a dark path.

"So, what do you think you gon' do with yo' life?" Tasha asked her with a drunken slur.

Reeses didn't answer but reacted with a face change.

"I'll tell you what's gonna happen. You're gonna earn ya way around here by any means. Understand?"

The tension in Reeses's body grew tighter as Tasha continued to speak.

"Real bad bitches do what they want. Busted hoes do what they can. I'm that bad bitch!" Tasha said, pointing at herself. "So, are you gonna be a busted hoe, Reeses, or will you be a boss like someone in yo' daddy's bloodline is supposed to be?"

The tears that sat in Reeses's eyes were tears of confusion. She didn't understand the conversation Tasha was having with her, but she knew it wasn't good. "My mama always said bitches who don't get with the picture get cut out. You're a beautiful girl. You were made to sit back and be taken care of. Don't be dumb, li'l girl. You gon' be what I want you to be. You hear me?" Tasha said in a low, raspy voice.

The chills that moved through Reeses's spine were a mark that would change her forever.

***

Ten years later

Pulling up to the curb of the parking lot, Reeses stepped out of the car and headed inside her house.

Walking in, she sat on the couch and pulled off her Christian Louboutin heels, placing them on the side of the coffee table. She got up and headed into the kitchen. The black tights she wore hugged her juicy bottom firmly while she stood flipping through the mail. Seeing the letter from the federal prison reminded her to slide some money on her brothers' accounts, even though they continued to tell her not to. There wasn't a week that went by that she didn't make sure they ate.

It was a long time coming from the position Reeses was left in. The only people she had left were her brothers and grandmother. If it wasn't for the pay masters on the street and Magic City, the world would be a shitty place in her eyes. The only thing Tasha pumped into her brain was getting a nigga out of a dollar. That statement was something that Tasha didn't live up to.

Around the summertime of last year, she was tricked into a nigga's bed, letting down her guards. Everything seemed perfect until the doctors told her she was HIV positive. There wasn't a day that went by that Reeses didn't think of the tragedy that had fallen upon the same woman who built her. It was sad to say, but Tasha turned her into a full time finesser. The game didn't come sweet, but it surely came with the ingredients. There was only one way to find out if a bitch was ready to be a boss: throw her to the streets and see if she climbed on top.

Reeses was only eighteen years old with the mind of a thirty-year-old hustler. Her chocolate skin and grey eyes complemented her sexy, curvy frame. Her waist was petite and she had an all-natural butt. Her dimples would pop out every time she showed her perfect thirty-two teeth. There wasn't one hustler in the hood that didn't want to have her. Being eighteen, but shaped like you were twenty-eight, would change a man's mind about how old she was.

Walking into her bathroom, Reeses stood in front of the mirror and released her jet-black hair out of its ponytail. She blew a kiss at herself in the mirror and licked her hot pink lips.

"Such a bad bitch," she mumbled, pulling out her cell.

Dialing a number, she placed it on speaker phone and set it on the marble white counter.

"Yo, wassup, li'l one?" a man answered in a calm voice.

"That's not my name, and I'm at home now. So, what was it you needed to talk about so bad earlier?"

"Damn, Reeses, you ain't always got to be an ass, and you know what I wanted to talk about. We been friends for a few months and I want to start putting a little extra step into seeing you."

"Men don't take steps. They act. I need a man who can give me everything I want."

"I'm willing to give up my last to a queen like you though. I'm trying to make this about you, Reeses."

"Exactly! If you give me everything, where does that leave you? If you gave me your last, that means you'll have nothing. What would be my point of staying if there's nothing left? I'm talking about men who would give me everything and still have enough to give me the rest of the world, sweetie."

"Why you always gotta be so deep, shawty? You know I have nothing but good intentions, girl."

"Yeah, well keep your intention on sending the $2,500 to my PayPal account. After that, you can get your date and see where it goes."

Hanging up, she turned on the hot water knob to the glass shower and peeled out of her clothes.

CHRIS GREEN

Chapter 4

It was an hour later when the Cadillac Escalade pulled in front of Reeses's home. Opening the passenger side door, she got in and closed it behind her.

"Damn, Reeses, you looking good today, ma. You just a hard woman to get in touch with." Fresh smiled with a light grin.

Fresh was a semi-rich nigga who was dibbing and dabbing in the city with his hands in everything. He was never a gangster. The only thing that clouded his mind was money - and of course, Reeses.

"Fresh, I already told you this ten times before. I'm not on that type of level with you yet. I think your ears are a little dirty, sweetie. See, I'm not the girl you're gonna jam your dick into. I come with a price of different needs."

"I'm starting to think you feel like I'm one of these other cats out here, Reeses. I can take care of you for the rest of your life. It's no such thing as having needs with me. All you have to do is relax and enjoy yourself."

"Money makes me enjoy myself."

Frowning up his face, he reached into his pocket and pulled out a wad of hundreds, dropping them into her lap.

"Since you keep hollering about paper, that should be enough for your time today, right? That's seven g's. Now can I at least pull you away from in front of your house? I can't show you better, if you don't know no better."

Reeses giggled at him, looking down at the bills. Cutting her eyes, she began to rub across her perfect breasts down to her juicy thighs.

"You're so thirsty, sweetheart. Is that all you think I'm worth, seven grand? I keep my time short and sacred because I'm the bitch you dream about pumping into every night.

When you start to understand that the world revolves around me, maybe you can feel the watery sweetness of these treats. Can I tell you something?"

Fresh's mouth was slightly hanging open with lust spilling from his face. "You can tell me anything, ma."

"The time for your seven grand has just run out."

Opening the door, she stepped out with the money in her hands. Thumbing through half of the bills, she counted out three thousand and tossed it back inside the window.

"That's four for you. The three is just for me wasting my breath. I'll see you later when you're ready to be the boss I know you can be."

Flashing a big smile, Fresh shook his head and turned on the ignition. He knew in his mind that it would take more than a few dollars to make her jump. Hands down she was a boss bitch, one that should be cherished. The thought of her screaming his name in bed caused him to chuckle as he pulled off. It was only a matter of time.

Climbing into her car, Reeses closed the door and watched Fresh leave out of her parking lot, heading in the opposite direction. Looking in the rearview mirror, she observed her surroundings until she got on the expressway.

***

Cosby Spears – High Rise Homes

Reeses began to slow down while she drove down North Avenue. Feeling her phone vibrate, she picked it up and placed it to her ear.

"Hello?"

"Bitch, where are you? I haven't heard from yo' ass all day."

Reeses laughed loudly into the phone as she turned into the elderly housing complex.

"Girl, shut the fuck up. You know I miss you, Dolly. I'm just over here by Boulevard to visit my granny real quick. Are you bringing your ass to work tonight?" Reeses replied.

"Girl, you know damn well Magic is the only thing that can make me smile. I need a little extra paper for my trip to Texas next week."

Reeses stepped out of the car, heading towards the building.

"Dolly, I told you if you need something, I will give it to you. Pull your pride out ya ass and take the money. At least you know everything will be good for the trip."

"Reeses, you know I'm not like that. Just because you're my girl and you got more money doesn't mean I'm gonna be a burden on you. I'ma see you at the club tonight, baby pop. We can talk about it then."

"Alright."

Placing the phone in her purse, Reeses walked in the entrance and signed in at the desk.

"Hey, Ms. Rivers. How are you?" the old nurse asked, walking through the main hall.

"I'm good, Ms. Adams," Reeses replied, waving her hand and making her way up to her grandmother's room.

She arrived in front of her door within thirty seconds and pressed the button to the buzzer. The sounds of the locks clicking allowed her entrance to the small apartment.

The smell of banana nut bread filled the air, as usual. As Reeses moved towards the living room, she saw a short, brown-skinned woman resting peacefully on the bed. Even though her head was full of grey hair, her bright smile made her look like she was forty instead of seventy-eight.

"Hey Nana. Why didn't you ask who it was before you buzzed the door, young lady?"

"Because, my love, you always come around this time of the evening. You better give me my hug, little girl."

Reeses tiptoed quickly to her side and planted a hard kiss on her cheek.

"You know I missed you, Nana. Why don't they have anyone in here to help you? They left you sitting in the bed like this?"

"Well, baby, I really don't have a choice. My bones just aren't working like they used to. You know that I'm always gonna be good no matter how bad the storm. I have the twenty-four hour service of my doctors. They come check in with me every hour."

"Nana, you can just let me help you."

"Reeses, you know I'm a one lady army. I'm fine. Did you get a chance to stop by the house?"

"Yes ma'am. I cleaned up a little like always and changed all of the locks yesterday."

"Baby, I know I been telling you this for a long time, but it's something that I have to give you. I know I had to wait for the perfect time. You have something waiting on you. I would handle things on my own, but unfortunately, I'm not in the best position. I need you to come by and see me tomorrow. It's important."

"Nana, I will come through here every day from now on. Tomorrow we can talk while I push you around in the gardens. You need air, and that's not going to happen being jammed in the bed all day."

"Listen, pumpkin, long as I got me some *Family Feud* and Tyler Perry movies, I'm in my heaven."

They both shared a laugh and talked for the next thirty minutes. After splitting a piece of cake, Reeses hugged her grandmother's neck and headed out to complete the rest of her day. It always hurt to see her only grandmother down on her last leg with her health. Her spirit and determination were the only thing that kept a huge smile inside of her heart.

Sitting on top of his Impala, the man watched as Reeses made her way to her car and got in. He was so amazed at the way she looked that it made him look twice. He couldn't help but smile as he watched her call pull away.

Standing up, he pulled his fitted cap down and headed inside the building. He looked at the sleeping security guard and walked directly past him. Walking through the hallway, he made his way upstairs to his destination and pressed the buzzer.

The door clicked and he walked inside.

***

Hearing the ring of her monitor, she pressed the button, hoping that Reeses didn't forget anything. Her smile was high and bright until she saw the man walk around the corner. Her joyful expression turned into a horrible frown.

"Hey, Mama. Why you look like you ain't happy to see me?" Slick said, walking to the side of her and taking a seat.

"Boy, I haven't seen you in almost eight months and you walk in here like you care about me. What do you want, Sheldon?"

Slick smiled, kissing her on the forehead. "Why you always think I want something, Mama? I am your son. It's not against the law for me to come check on you, is it?"

"Boy, when you care anything about the law? You must have forgot who you talking to."

"Did you see your niece? She just left out right before you arrived."

"Nah, I didn't see her," Slick lied quickly.

The mention of Reeses made him spark the conversation he badly wanted.

"Isn't she like eighteen now? I know Jimmie left her a lot of money behind. So, what is she doing for herself?" he said a little too anxiously.

"Whatever Jimmie left her is between him and his daughter. She has her head on straight. So whatever she do is gonna help her live the life she needs to."

"Mama, you been sittin' around carrying all this money around for Jimmie ever since he died. You did it for what? Your medical bills and health issues aren't even covered. You ain't even taking care of yourself, but you can drag money around for a stupid teenager who gonna do some stupid shit with it, like spend it on nothing. I heard Jimmie left her two million dollars. Why would something like that be left out from the family knowing?"

"I wouldn't give a damn if he left her eight million, it isn't none of your business. Jimmie did everything in his power to make sure that girl wanted for nothing. Now what does this have to do with the family? You've never been interested in us any time before."

"Your almighty Jimmie took all the vision from your old eyes. All you cared about was making sure he was happy instead of your biological son. If this was ever a family, I never got the correct impression. All I'm trying to do is help you. You can tell me where it is, and I can take care of you and the family the right way. She's too young and you know she'll need our help," he replied, trying to make sense out of the trickery.

"Slick, you're my son, and I love you very much, but your intentions aren't good, son. I'm gonna make sure that girl stays away from you. If she fails, it will be on her own, not because we wanted to control anything. All you need to do is let her find out what she wants to do on her own and be happy for her."

The crooked smile he wore on his face showed his anger. Sucking on his teeth, he nodded his head, standing up. "You right, Ma. At the end of the day, I just want you to know I love you."

Leaning down, he kissed her forehead and snatched the pillow from under her head, placing it over her face. He began to apply pressure as she jerked violently. Her weak bones weren't a match for the strong hands that gripped around her face.

"Just rest, Mama, please," Slick mumbled, pressing down harder on the pillow.

The tussling and jerking stopped when the cries faded to her last breath.

Taking the pillow from her face, Slick propped it back behind her head and straightened it out quickly.

Looking around the small room, nothing but silence filled the air. He stared down at his mother's lifeless body and took a deep breath.

"I need this, and I can't have you in my way," he said in a light voice and then he walked out the door.

CHRIS GREEN

Chapter 5

The atmosphere of Magic City glistened through the streets of the city brightly. Gangstas down to the street hustlers were attending the movement. It was normal for a half a million dollars to be thrown on the right night inside the strip bar.

Moving towards the private dance section, Slick grabbed ahold of Dolly's hand as she walked past him.

"Hey baby, you sure is moving fast for somebody who's trying to get that money."

Dolly flashed a small smile. She placed her hand on the side of her hip. Her brown skin complexion glowed perfectly under the colored lights.

"It's only 11:00 at night. I gotta move twice as fast now to reach this quota, sugar."

"Who was the girl I seen you with like twenty minutes ago?" Slick added in quickly.

"Who you talking about? Her?" Dolly asked, pointing across the room to Reeses on the small stage.

The small thong she wore was swallowed inside of her soft cheeks while she twerked slowly. Her jet black hair hung down her back in a ponytail and the small mask that covered her grey eyes made her look even more provocative when she arched her back and looked at the crowd.

"That's my girl Reeses. Let me guess: you want me to go get her over here, huh? Everybody's always requesting her."

"Nah, li'l mama. Nothing like that. I just wondered who she was to you. Fuck her, let's talk about you," Slick said, puling Dolly onto his lap.

Grabbing onto her petite waist, he slipped five crispy hundreds inside her leg loop. Placing his hand on her ass, he gripped firmly as she started to move off the music playing.

"How come I never seen you in here before? I've been working here a while. It's not too many people that's spending a half a grip on a dance. Maybe Big Meech, but definitely not a local joker."

Slick smiled, looking into her eyes. Young Thug's single "Givenchy" played loudly while she continued to grind her hips into his crotch.

"I'm not a local joker from any city or state and money only means something to people who care about it. So, are you gonna tell me the price or not?" Slick asked, looking at the thin layer of material that covered her pussy lips.

"What makes you think you got enough for a chick like me? I'm not the first fish that bites the rod when you throw it inside the water."

"It's not about the first one that bites. It's about how many you can catch. First, I want to have something to eat and then make you spazz out on the dick, and judging from how fat that coochie is, you probably a squirter."

"I see you got jokes. I charge $900.00 for a night and I don't do dicks under eight inches. You think you can rock with that, big baller?" Dolly questioned, feeling the bulge in his pants.

"What time will you be ready?"

"If you give me like ten minutes to grab my things, I will meet you outside."

Kissing the side of her neck, he stood up, looking down at her magnificent shape.

"I'm in the black Chrysler 300."

"I drive the white Lexus coupe that's parked next to you. You can just follow me back to my place."

"Don't keep me waiting," Slick mumbled, walking off with his head low under the lights.

Making her way through the dance floor, Dolly headed back to the locker room to collect her bags.

Reeses was fully changed into her street clothes by the time Dolly turned the corner.

"Damn, bitch! You already leaving?"

"Girl, my performance ended when a nigga offered that check for this ass. Money has to be made one way or another, baby."

Reeses laughed lightly while Dolly quickly got dressed.

"What lucky trick is you about to finesse, Dolly?"

"The lucky one who asked to be tricked. Money don't got no face. It's just how quick you can handle that to get them on they way. One nut for each squirrel."

"I don't blame you, boo. Be careful and call me whenever you get settled in."

"I got you, baby mama."

Grabbing her Chanel purse, Dolly made her way to the front entrance. Walking towards her car, she looked over at Slick sitting in his driver seat. Giving him a small smile, she hopped inside and pulled off with Slick directly behind her.

***

It was around 12:45 when Dolly stepped out of the car in front of the house. Strolling to the side of Slick's whip, she opened the passenger door and got in.

"I'ma let you know now before I let you in my house, I'm not with the whole lovey dovey thing. It's strictly business," Dolly said, looking at him seriously.

"What's understood, doesn't need to be explained."

Nodding her head, she opened the door to step back out.

Grabbing her by the pants, Slick snatched her back inside. The psychotic look on his face told her that he had a total different plan.

"Nigga, what the fuck is wrong with you!" she yelled, trying to get away from his grasp.

The 9 mm that slammed into her face caused stars to flare up in her vision. She instantly began to pour tears as he moved closer, covering her mouth.

"First off, I need you to shut the fuck up and listen to me really good. Do you understand me?"

Her eyes grew wide in fear while she prayed that he would do whatever he had to and leave.

"I'm gonna ask you one time only. Please do not make me shoot you. I want to know where Reeses is laying her head. Give me the address," he demanded, gripping the pistol tightly.

***

The sun shone brightly the next morning. The chirping of the birds caused Reeses to open her eyes slowly.

When she rose from the bed, the only things that covered her body were see-through boy shorts and a matching bra. Arching her back for a good stretch, she moved towards the dresser as her phone began to ring.

"Hello?"

"Ms. Rivers, this is the head care holder at Cosby Spears nursing home. It's about your grandmother," the male stated through the phone.

"What about my grandmother?" Reeses asked with her heart jumping a mile a minute.

"Your grandmother passed away last night. I'm so sorry, ma'am. We have her belongings packed if you would like to come pick them up."

The remark was like a knife ripping through her heart. Reeses dropped to her knees and the tears began to pour while she held the phone.

"Ms. Rivers, we know that this is a tragic moment for you. The home is paying the full cost for her funeral and we will be behind you through this entire process. We can mail the property to you if you'd like, free of charge."

"That's okay, sir, I'll come by and pick everything up now," Reeses replied, setting the touchscreen on the floor.

Rubbing her hands through her hair, she wiped the tears from her face. The last person who was close to her had just been pulled away in the blink of an eye. The love and care that her grandmother gave were irreplaceable. Losing her was never gonna sit right.

Standing up off the floor, she headed to the bathroom and quickly showered. After getting out, she put on her grey Chanel sweat suit, slid on her black Nike slippers, walked out, and made her way over to the nursing home.

It took an entire hour to get away from the old citizens who were friends with Ms. Lester. The sad stories and loving moments they started to share got too emotional for Reeses, causing her to leave as soon as she could. After placing four boxes of her granny's things in the backseat, she left the lot with sadness in her heart, knowing there was no returning.

Since she was not too far away from her grandmother's house, she decided to stop by and clear out the important things and prepare for her funeral. It felt strange only being eighteen and having the world placed on your shoulders. It was hard, and losing her dad and mom at eight years old had turned her beautiful soul into a cold stone.

It was twenty minutes later when she pulled down Fifth Street in front of the beige home. The butterflies began to come through her stomach when she stepped out of the car. Grabbing all the boxes, she made her way inside and closed the door.

The aura of the house gave off the energy of a real family home. Tons of pictures lined the walls and mantel. The green couch set blended perfectly with the white walls and the white rug on the floor.

Setting the stuff on the coffee table, she sat on the couch, taking a deep breath.

The flashes of her grandma couldn't help but pop into her head. The hurt of not being able to talk to her anymore made the pain even deeper.

Grabbing one of the boxes, she opened the lid and began to look through her personal items. The framed picture of her mother that sat on the side caught her eye when she removed the black photo album. Picking it up, she stared at the woman she use to call Mom. It was hard to understand at a young age, but as she got older, she realized Sharon had let drugs ruin the last piece of life she obtained. Feeling the disgust build inside of her, Reeses's hand lunged forward and she threw the picture against the brick fireplace.

A silver bracelet flew out of the frame and landed on the floor, making her heart stop. She walked towards it, looking down at her mom's matching bracelet. The half a heart resembled the same one that was currently dangling on her wrist. It was a horrible flashback as she remembered the day her mom was rolled out of their house on a stretcher. The last time she saw it was over nine years ago as a child. Spotting a folded piece of paper hanging in the frame, she grabbed it, shaking the glass on the floor. Unfolding it, she looked at the paper closely and began to read.

"Rinesha,

I know that sometimes growing up in a world where it feels everything is going against you will make you feel alone. Even at an old age I, as your grandmother, know you will be everything you are meant to be. There are more blessings you haven't counted, and your father made me promise to wait until you got older to tell you. His words were the last thing I heard before he was murdered when you were just a child. I hope that I can live long enough to see you explore this world. If I can't, I will know you are set for the rest of your life. Hold your mother's bracelet close to you and find your new life, baby.

Love always,
Grandma
P.S. Look on the heart."

The confusing letter scrambled Reeses's mind as she stood in place. Looking at the bracelet in her hands, she turned it over, looking at the words engraved in the middle.

"Base?"

The word twisted her brain even more until she looked on the back of her own. Taking it off her wrist, she placed them together and stared at it awkwardly.

It spelled out the word "basement" in bold letters.

Scratching her head, she wondered how the marking could be skipped over for so long. The bracelet rarely came off her arm, but the words on the back had always been a mystery. Repeating it over in her head made the thought of the key to downstairs pop up. Pulling it out of her pocket, she stared at it and walked towards the hallway.

The thought of the new lock she placed on the door a week ago caused her antenna to rise. It was even weirder because her grandmother forced her to hold onto the key for dear life.

Opening the lock, she pushed the door open and looked down the dark steps that led to the bottom floor. Her heartbeat started to thump as she took her first step.

Chapter 6

The thick cold air in the basement caused Reeses to rub her arms to adjust. Flicking on the light switch, she looked around the wooden walls and dull scenery. The old model television that sat on the floor was full of dust around the screen and the raggedy pull out sofa reeked of cheap cigarettes.

She started to quickly move around the room, searching everything she possibly could. Her hope began to run dry until she stood face to face with the giant rock band poster that hung on the wall. The four men with the guitars didn't intrigue her, but the large broken heart at the top did. Stepping closer, she read the words at the center of the paper.

"Tears from my heart?"

Placing her hand against it, she rubbed across the hard surface slowly. The edge of her nail scratched a small hole through the frail poster, leaving a dark black spot.

Pausing, she looked harder and pulled off another piece. The thin tape caused the rest of the poster to fall gently to the floor, exposing the black steel safe. Her mouth hung wide open. She pushed a layer of hair from her vision.

Trying to keep her brain from racing, she began to turn a number onto the combination. Pulling on the handle, she realized that her birthday wasn't the code. It took her ten tries before she started to get aggravated. Kicking the poster made a lightbulb fly on top of her head when she looked down.

Tears from my heart - 11/12/06.

Staring at the numbers, she began to enter them in slowly. Hearing the loud click made chills run through her fingers. As the air from the pressure-sealed safe escaped, she pulled it open and froze in place as she looked inside. She had always wondered why her grandmother would purchase a new home that she was barely in, or why she was so caught up on making sure it was clean and safe when no one was ever around.

Taking a step back, Reeses's eyes wandered from top to bottom. Bundles of thick cash filled the entire space except for the kilos of cocaine that sat on top. Her paranoia started to surface as she looked around the room. She felt that she was being watched. Picking up a wad of the cash, she flipped quickly through the bills, estimating an easy ten thousand. From the looks of the rest inside, she knew that there had to be at least a million dollars.

One thing she knew for sure, mathematics in school wasn't as hard as it seemed. When it came to numbers, Reeses was more of an expert than a trained accountant.

Wasting no time, she grabbed the rolling suitcase and pulled it in front of her. The bundles of money fell into the bag heavily while she rushed to grab everything inside. Clearing the safe out in under thirty seconds, she zipped up the bag and dragged it upstairs. The mission she had on her agenda was to get the hell out of the house immediately.

Stepping out on the porch, she locked the front door to the crib and slowly walked to the car. Just the thought of throwing the case in the backseat gave her goosebumps.

Getting inside her car, she wasted no time letting her tires speak. Her mind was saying to call Dolly, but that best friend of hers would only spill the shit to the entire city before she got to the house. Changing her plans quickly, she knew one person who would never trade on her for anything in the world.

***

As she came down her street, the car door was open before Reeses could hit the brakes. She was speeding so quickly that she hopped out of the whip in her bare feet. It was best to move quietly and quickly in the Smyrna, Georgia area. The neighbors always had the tendency to put their noses in other people's business.

Getting inside the house, she placed the suitcase on the kitchen table and poured out the cash. Looking at the blessing, her mind wandered to where she was gonna hide it. Something just didn't feel right with it sitting out.

Quickly placing it back inside the bag, she looked out her living room curtains before she walked out the door and across the street.

***

The knock on the front door broke Beno's concentration from the Pyrex bowl he was about to place on the stove. Setting it on the countertop, he walked inside his living area swiftly.

Seeing Reeses's face always sent chills through his body. His love ran deeper than an ocean for her, but only so much was accepted.

"Hey, Beno. Are you busy?"

Looking into her beautiful eyes he smiled, stepping to the side and allowing her entrance.

"Reeses, where have you been? For you to be my best friend, you sure do break a lot of promises."

"Don't do that, Beno. You know I work a lot, and things have been going really wrong lately."

"I've been your friend since middle school. Any problem you've ever had, I gave all the help that was possible. You're stubborn - just like you were five years ago," Beno said, reaching into his fridge.

"Boy, shut the hell up. You know I will neva trade on you. You're my headache, but you're my friend."

"My point exactly: your friend," Beno replied, handing her a pack of Reeses cups.

Beno stood six feet even with a low temp fade that made him look younger then he was. His teeth were perfectly white and his athletic build complemented his height. He was hardly ever mad and he would remind you of Terence J from B.E.T. His eyes always set low, making him look as if he smoked a pound of marijuana, but his voice told you that he was more of a good guy then he seemed.

Seeing the candy made her blush and flash a bright smile. The look in his eyes moistened the inside of her panties as she stood in front of him. Kissing his cheek lightly, she rubbed her hand through his waves.

"Beno, you're so sweet. If we weren't friends, I would let you take my virginity, but unfortunately, men are dogs and I refuse to lose a good friendship for taking a chance. You know you're still number one." Reeses giggled sexily.

Her mind was really scared of relationships after witnessing how her mother had been dragged through the mud. She knew that a man could switch at any time and rather than lose a best friend, she would just support him and keep things mutual.

Beno couldn't help but laugh at her arrogance. Ever since he first laid eyes on her as a young teenager, he was hooked. The love that he was ready to offer was true in his heart, but not good enough to make Reeses put her guard down.

"So, what's been going on?" he asked, making his way back in front of the kitchen stove.

"My grandmother passed away this morning. I just found out a few hours ago. Besides my brothers, she was all I had left."

"Damn, Reeses, I'm so sorry about that. I didn't mean to be all in yo' grill about being around. I know how you feel about your grandmother. Is there anything I can do to help out?"

"Nah, not really. I'm preparing her funeral for next week. After that, I was thinking about opening up a few businesses and getting the hell away from here."

Shaking his head, Beno placed the glass pot over the fire. "You know if you ever need me, I'll be glued to the same spot, waiting for you."

Reeses sat in silence, watching him pull the baking soda box out of his kitchen cabinet. Making her way beside him, she looked over his shoulder as he watched the water slowly turn to a boil.

"Dang, nosy. Why is you all in the kitchen around these felonies? You don't like seeing me do wrong. Remember?"

"Boy, I will kick you in yo' ass. You been a fuck up when it comes to trouble. Now what the hell are you doing?"

Beno gave Reeses an aggravated face as he dumped seven grams of cocaine inside the third of water. Grabbing the baking soda, he carefully shook it over the pot, blending the mix up with the drugs. Grabbing a metal fork, he lifted the pot up and began to stir it with a fast whip-like motion after a few minutes passed. The small splotches of cocaine started to form together. Dipping his hand in the cold water next to him, he splashed a few drops inside and continued to whip.

Reeses watched carefully as he placed his hand in the Pyrex. Pulling out the small, formed cookies of dope, he laid them gently on three brown napkins and washed his hands.

"So, is this why I haven't been seeing you work at the Wayfield lately? Because you been selling crack?" Reeses asked with a disgusted face.

"It's not like that. I already told you a few months back that money is getting kinda tight. I just do it for a little extra paper. It's not really a big deal."

"I also told you months ago that if you needed anything, I would help you, Beno. You're good at claiming we're best friends, but when I offer you help financially, you shut me out."

"Because I'm a man, Reeses. You're the same way. I offered you help with numerous situations and you closed me down. 'Cause why? Maybe your bank account is already loaded. I know I couldn't possibly do anything in that area. You're probably one of the prettiest women walking around this city, so being with a local nigga like me is below your standards. Now that I think about it, I've never been accepted with nothing I try to offer towards you. The hurt is all because of you."

Walking in his face, her right hand slammed against his right cheek.

"How dare you speak to me on some weak-ass stuff like that? Who was by your side in middle school when everyone made you out to be a duck? Who turned other niggas around when you had no one to go to the prom with? You've been accepted on everything with my life since the sixth grade, Beno. Just because I have personal problems dealing with my family doesn't mean that I can't offer you help if you're struggling."

Looking in her face, he could tell he put a little too much into his words. The slight tears in her eyes indicated that her sensitive button had been pushed.

"I'm sorry, Reeses. I know you could help me with any problem that I have, but in the end, I'm still a man. I wouldn't feel right if I had to always call on you. I hate doing wrong, but I don't have any choice unless you don't want me to survive."

"You don't have to take a risk getting drugs out the street. You can always call me to handle things too. What the fuck are friends for?"

He couldn't help but laugh at Reeses's stubbornness. Her ways were more like a caring sister or mother instead of a friend. That was the care that caused him to love her more than she understood.

"Now I know you can help me and all, but you can't help me with nothing dealing with any drugs, girl," Beno said, making his way back to the kitchen counter.

"What gives you that bright-ass idea? I know a little more than you think I do."

"Really? Please do tell."

"I don't tell, I show. I know if you want some, then I can give it to you."

Beno busted out into laughter again before he grabbed his blunt off the coffee table. His smile began to fade as he realized she was beyond serious.

"Reeses, you know I care for you. I don't think you on point with shit that's going on in the trap. It's a whole different level. You know that I'm talking about cocaine, right?"

Looking at him with a quick smirk, Reeses walked out of the front door.

"Rees, I was just asking a question. Don't get mad at me," Beno said, trying to walk behind her.

The front door closed in his face, leaving him in the living room alone. Shaking his head, he sat down on the couch and lit the fat spliff. Inhaling hard, he sat back and began to think. Blowing out a cloud full of smoke, his thoughts were cut short when Reeses walked back through the door with a small black trash bag.

Sitting quietly, he remained on the sofa while she made her way towards him. She threw it on the table and Beno's eyes widened when he saw the bricks slide on the raggedy wooden top. Picking one up, he looked directly into her eyes.

"Reeses, where did you get this?"

"Mm-hmm, I told you, nigga. Don't ever doubt me," she replied arrogantly.

Pulling out his small box cutter, he punctured the plastic, exposing the crystal-like powder. Dipping his pinky finger in, he rubbed it across his gums lightly. Feeling the numbness that invaded his mouth, he began to twitch his face.

"This shit is pure as fuck. I can't even feel my fucking jaw. Where did this come from?"

"I found it ducked off in my grandma's spot. I think it might have belonged to one of my brothers."

"Reeses, this is five bricks. Do you know how much we can make off this?"

"I don't know, genius. That's for you to know and find out. If this is what's gonna get you on your feet, at least you will be toting enough to really make you some paper."

Flashing a giant smile, he got up and wrapped her into a big hug. The quick kisses he placed on her cheek made her giggle with excitement.

"Boy, get yo' ass off me. You gon' wrinkle my clothes."

"Listen, I fucking love you. I promise we can split everything down the middle."

"I don't wanna split anything. I wanna see you take off and make sure I'm straight forever."

"I promise you everything will be good from here on out."

"Well, get started. I need to prepare for my grandmother's funeral. I gotta head out to work tonight. I guess I'll catch up with you tomorrow," Reeses said, headed for the door.

"You know I got you. Please do not get lost on me this time."

Smiling, she threw up the deuces and walked out.

Chapter 7

Reeses grinded slowly down the pole, popping her Georgia peach slowly. Young Thug's "Single Pacifier" played loudly through the tall pro speakers. Thirsty niggas in the club wasted no time throwing their entire bank roll at her apple bottom. Smiling with a devilish grin, she slid down into a perfect split, grabbing a pile of bills. Her performance lasted for two more minutes and she made her way off the stage.

As she made her way through the crowd a hand reached out, grabbing her arm lightly. Turning around quickly she looked at Fresh, who was standing like he was the king of the city. His Audemers watch glistened brightly and the snapback he wore hung low over his eyes.

"Why does it seem like you get badder every time I see you?" he asked, smiling and showing off his dimples.

Reeses couldn't help but smile as she pulled her arm away.

"Boy, you just don't quit, do you? How did you know I even worked tonight?" she asked with a curious face.

"It's not too many things I can't figure out about you. I know when you dance you zone out in your own world. I know you hate to be told what to do, and I know you hate people that are easy to give up. You hate to be played with, but your swag shows you truly want to be loved."

Fresh could tell that his words hit a certain spot from her arrogant smirk.

"That all sounds very good, but there's a lot that comes behind that huge word. How you know that li'l love you feeling in your chest ain't just lust?"

"Sometimes you have to take chances to see. Love is an opportunity, but you also gotta know when that chance is worth taking. All I ask for is one date. If you aren't comfortable after that, I'll fall back until you decide otherwise," he said in a sincere tone.

Tilting his hat to the side, she winked her eye and blew him a kiss.

"You definitely have a better chance now than you did with the first approach. I know how to reach you," she replied, heading off to the locker room.

Fresh grinned with a cheesy smile, rubbing his goatee. He watched her ass move from side to side as she disappeared through the blocked off section.

***

Preparing her things to leave the club, Reeses looked at the clock on her phone. It read 11:46 p.m. Scrolling through her call log, she clicked Dolly's name and placed it to her ear.

The first ring sent her straight to the voicemail. Clicking her name again, she received the same results and placed her phone back in her Gucci bag. Sliding on her Balmain slippers, she made her way out of the club to the car.

Thinking about Dolly made her feel weird. It wasn't like her to miss out on celebrity guest night. There were guaranteed thousands to be made, so missing out was kind of against the rules. Knowing her friend, she was probably relapsed with laziness from whatever stranger's dick she received the other night.

Laughing to herself, Reeses decided to head over to her house. It wasn't long before she arrived at the two bedroom house on Dill Avenue. Seeing Dolly's car, Reeses pulled in directly next to hers. Cutting the engine, she stepped out and headed to her porch. She knocked on the door a few times and waited patiently for an answer. Looking inside the front window, it seemed as if no one was home.

Reeses backed off the front steps, walked to Dolly's car, and looked through the glass. Her Jimmie Choo heels rested on the passenger side floor and the car looked like it hadn't been moved in days.

"If this bitch left on vacation and didn't tell, I'ma be pissed," Reeses mumbled.

Getting back in her car, she pulled off and headed to her house.

***

Reeses headed inside her home as she checked her phone notifications. Clicking the PayPal app, she laughed upon seeing the $2500 that had recently been added to her account. Now she knew it was true that people would pay you without even seeing your face.

Tapping on the message from Beno, she dialed his number quickly after reading the words "call me".

"Hello?"

"Beno, what's wrong? I seen you tell me to call," Reeses asked.

"This dope is what's wrong. I've been on the eastside ever since you left me earlier and gotten rid of two already. The shit is so good, the nigga bought 'em from me wholesale. Reeses, I made seventy grand in ten hours. This stuff is like ninety percent pure."

Hearing seventy grand caused her to pause.

"How in the hell did you just make that much money in just hours?"

"Listen, I don't know where your people got this from, but all I can tell you is if we get our hands on anymore or find a plug with something just as good, we will be rich. I've never seen anything like this. I came to one of my people's spots earlier and gave him a little to brush off for me. The shit was gone within one hour.

"Stop! Let's not say too much and just wait until I can see you tomorrow. We will have to put our heads together and think of something."

"Cool, I'll see you in the a.m."

Hanging up the phone, she sat on the couch, thinking of what she had just been told. The giant lightbulb that popped in the top of her head caused her to take off to the bathroom. Going inside the closet, she came back out with six Nike shoeboxes. Setting them on the bed, she opened them all one by one and poured everything out.

Looking at all the wads of cash, she dug in and began to count. Her eyes concentrated on the bills as she thumbed through them quickly in silence. It took less than fifteen minutes for her to count out a hundred grand.

Smiling from ear to ear, she placed the money back and grabbed her phone. Pressing the call button, she waited as it rang in her ear.

"Hey, beautiful. To what do I owe to this call?" Fresh asked as he picked up.

"You owe everything to it if you let me decide. I need to talk to you. Do you think you can come over here or not?" Reeses asked seriously.

"I'll be there in twenty minutes," he said, quickly hanging up.

Seeing that her plan was much easier than she thought, Reeses made her way to the shower and bathed quickly. After getting out, she slid on her small white Gucci shorts. Throwing on a V-neck T-shirt, she applied her Paris Hilton lotion and combed through her hair. The doorbell ringing made her move swiftly to the front of the house. Opening the door, she smirked at Fresh leaning on the side of her wall.

"Boy, who the hell are you supposed to be? Denzel? Come in," Reeses said, moving to the side.

"Good evening to you too," Fresh replied, walking past her into the house.

Locking the front door, she walked over to him, standing in the middle of the room.

"You gotta beautiful little spot here, ma. I see you got a little flavor. I'ma let you decorate our new dream home."

"You sure do move too fast. Do you want something to drink or what?"

"Sure, do you have Patron?"

"I got whatever you want," she said, making her way inside the kitchen.

Fixing the refreshments, she made her way back into the family room. Handing him his drink, she took a seat on the opposite couch across from him.

"So wassup, ma? You finally decide to let me get a little time with you?"

"You can say that. I wanna get to know you more, but I also need your help," Reeses said, trying to get straight to the point.

"What are you talking about? Is everything okay?"

"No, I'm trying to make something happen and I know you're the man to get it done."

"And what exactly is it that you're trying to handle?" he asked with a strange face.

"I need some dope."

"Excuse me? Did you say dope?"

Reeses took a sip of her drink as she nodded her head slowly.

"You mean like cocaine?"

"Yes, I mean cocaine. What the fuck else would I mean?"

"I'm sorry. I didn't know you used that shit, mama."

"Don't ever insult me like that again. I don't do drugs period, jackass. If you wanna put ya nose all in my business, I'm trying to make me some money."

"Oh shit! That's what's good. What you need? I gotta couple of zips at the house. I can take care of you on that ASAP," he said arrogantly.

"Don't take this the wrong way, but I make the value of a few ounces in a lap dance on a bad night. I don't think you have enough to take care of what I need. I want to meet the plug who you are getting it from."

Fresh looked at her with a blank face before he started to laugh.

"What the fuck seems to be funny?" Reeses asked, feeling as if he took her for a joke.

"I'm not laughing at you. I'm laughing at what you said. Meet the plug? My connect only handles weight. He's not about to meet you for a couple of thousand. I'm keeping it real because I really fuck with you."

"A couple of thousand may be your spending range. Like I said, I have some money to spend and I want weight," she said sternly.

"What exactly are you trying to spend?" Fresh asked, sitting up with a raised eyebrow.

"A hundred thousand. Maybe more."

"You wanna spend a hundred grand on dope? Are you serious?"

"As a fucking heart attack."

Taking a deep breath, Fresh pulled his phone from his coat pocket. Typing a number on the screen, he pressed the call button and placed it on speaker phone. It rang twice before the voice spoke through the line.

"What is it?" a man said in a thick Cuban accent.

"José. Sorry for the late call, but I know the news I have isn't an offer you would refuse," Fresh spoke with much respect.

"I'm listening," he replied in an unpleasant tone.

"I have someone who's very important to me who needs help. Of course, every minute will be worth the numbers that are in your category. I'm quite positive that you will be happy with this new business that will benefit you greatly."

"I'll see you tomorrow at nine o'clock in the morning. If you're a second late, I will cancel the meeting and see you next month as usual," José said before ending the call.

Fresh flashed a quick smile and knocked down the rest of his drink.

"You say you got a hundred you wanna spend? We heading out in the a.m. Please don't make me look bad on this."

Walking over to him, she gave him a tight hug and sat down. "Now that's the movement I need, sir. You did good."

Grabbing her hand, he kissed it lightly. "Anything is possible when it comes to making you happy. All you have to do is ask. Your beauty, your smile, your arrogance...that's what keeps me coming back. Can you fault a nigga for wanting a boss bitch such as yourself?"

Before Reeses could reply, Fresh pushed her back on the couch, spreading her legs. Sliding her shorts to the side, he buried his face in her pretty pussy lips before she could object.

Her actions ceased when he wrapped his lips around her clit. Sucking slow and soft, he moved his head from top to bottom.

Reeses's eyes began to roll. Her mind was caught in the feeling until Fresh raised up to unbutton his pants.

"Hold on, jackrabbit. I'm not ready for all of that right now. Can we please take this little thing slow and handle the business first?" Reeses asked, fixing her clothes.

She knew one thing for sure. A man who tries his best to get in your pants for some ass will eventually end up leaving you just for that: some ass. Her status as a self-made chick was not about to be tarnished by a man who only wanted to stick his dick in every pretty pussy he saw. She only let it move so far because of the small favor he was doing for her, nothing more. Men had a tendency to think with their privates instead of their brains and she knew that would wreck the entire plan that was set in her mind. Fresh was just a key that hadn't been turned until that very night

Wiping his mouth, Fresh smiled and licked his lips.

"Now that I know you taste as delicious as you look, I hope you can at least think about giving us a try."

"I don't take tries on anything but my money. Business before pleasure. It's just the way I rock."

"On the strength of you being so beautiful, I'll take that." Standing up, he fixed his clothes while staring her in the eyes. "I guess that concludes our night. We have a meeting very early. Please be ready," Fresh said as he blew her a kiss and headed out the door.

Locking up the house, Reeses giggled while she headed back to the shower.

Playing with someone's head was the number one rule. You only give so much. It was never meant to give full vulnerability. Placing the plan together in her head, she scratched off another job done. It was sad how easy one could be tricked, but playing the game was only about one thing: winning.

Chapter 8

Reeses stood in the morning breeze with her trench coat pulled closed. Just when her patience was about to run thin, Fresh pulled in front of the house in his Cadillac Escalade. Making her way towards the truck, she got in and slammed the door. Looking at her watch, she snapped quickly.

"You kicking all this boss man exclusive shit and you twenty minutes late on picking me up." Setting the duffle bag on the car floor, she crossed her legs and strapped on her seatbelt.

"Well good morning to you too," Fresh replied as he pulled off.

The drive to Forest Park, GA wasn't very long. You could tell from the change of scenery that the community wasn't based on the average income. It was truly a side where the grass was much greener. The Nissans and Toyotas were replaced with the latest Maserati and BMW's. The government-issued homes were swapped with half a million dollar cribs or better. Their journey came to a halt as they pulled in front of an exquisite six bedroom home. The camera above the gate obviously was watching because the gate opened immediately.

Pulling inside, Fresh parked next to a 1976 Corvette original. The paint was so clear that you could see the reflection of everything as he stopped the car.

"Now before we go in here, let me do the talking and I can make sure you walk out of here satisfied."

Reeses tooted her lips, ignoring every word while she climbed out of the vehicle. They made their way towards the house. She strutted with confidence until Fresh knocked on the door.

They waited for a brief moment, then the door to the house unlocked and opened. Reeses looked over at Fresh and he shrugged his shoulders, walking inside.

Reeses gasped, looking at the champagne gold walls and the antique statues. There were even small statuettes lined along the hallway leading to a bigger part of the mini mansion.

José stood as they made their way inside his large living area.

"José, it's a pleasure to be here. How are you, my friend?" Fresh asked, shaking the man's hand.

José's face was stern, but welcoming. "The pleasure is always mine. It has to be very important if you're willing to meet with me early in the a.m.," he replied in his thick Cuban accent. Dusting off his brown Versace slacks, he looked at his gold and brown Breitling watch and sat down. "You're here on time. You got fifteen minutes."

"Sir, the business I have for you won't take anything but half of that." Grabbing Reeses's arm, he pulled her lightly in front of him. "José, this is Reeses."

Flashing her a smile, José rose to his feet again and shook her small hand. "How are you, Reeses? To what do I owe this pleasure of meeting a young woman as beautiful as yourself?"

Pulling her bag off the shoulder, she set it down in front of him without saying a word.

Staring her in the eyes, he reached for the bag and opened the strings. Glimpsing the rolls of money, José closed the bag and sat up straight. "Is there something I'm missing?"

"No, there's nothing to miss. You agreed to meet with me and I set a hundred grand on your table the next morning."

Choosing his words carefully, José looked over at Fresh. "I'm lost. Do you care to explain?"

"It's easy. You're the man I needed to see for some product. I brought a hundred thousand plus an extra ten for even having this discussion. According to Fresh, your time is worth money. I'm hoping with that we can get off to a good start."

"Fresh, if you don't mind, I would like to speak to Reeses alone," Jose replied, looking at her dark grey eyes.

"No problem, sir."

Standing up, he walked through the double doors, closing them behind him.

"Do you have any idea what you're doing here?"

"If I didn't, I wouldn't be standing right here," Reeses replied.

"You're kind of arrogant for someone who throws a measly hundred thousand on my table. That's only ten percent of what I make a month. How do you know you can even afford what I have?"

"It's plenty more where that came from."

José flashed a smile. Reaching for his pack of smokes, he lit a cigarette and sat back. "My kilos are $25,000 apiece. I give them to Fresh for seventeen a block. If he buys six or more, fifteen. You have 100K, which means you get four."

"Fuck the prices you give to Fresh. Forget about $25,000, because that wouldn't be worth the hustle. This is just the beginning of what I have to offer. If it goes right, I'll be back with that times five. I'm trying to make moves, not sit on the block."

"If you don't mind me asking, how old are you?" José questioned.

"Old enough to know how to handle this business. I've never been good with the question thing either, no disrespect."

"None taken. For a woman, you have a lot of courage to come and speak men's business with me. You say what you feel. I respect that. I'll give them to you for twelve apiece. Hopefully, that can get the movement started for you. If good business is handled, I will supply you with everything you need from here on out," José spoke, putting his cigarette filter in the ashtray.

Even though José usually wouldn't trust an outsider so quickly, he had known Fresh for a long time and knew he wasn't going to lead him in the wrong direction when it came to his business. For some reason, he had a good feeling about the new clientele.

"I promise you won't be disappointed."

Shaking his hand, she sealed the deal and checked her next move off the list.

***

Walking out of José's crib, Reeses felt like the queen of Georgia. Holding her head high, she made her way to the truck, where Fresh stood looking clueless.

"What happened? Do you need me to go back in for you?"

"No, I handled my business. We can go now," Reeses said, jumping in the car with the duffle bag full of work.

"What do you mean you handled your business? I thought he just wanted to ask you a few questions. What did he say about the supply?"

"It's always good when it comes to me. I told him what I needed to, and he trusted my word. I think we are gonna be good business partners."

"How much did he give you?"

"A whole lot of nothing that ain't yo' business. I was always told that business isn't supposed to be spoke on. Don't you agree?"

"Yeah, sure," Fresh mumbled with a pissed expression.

The rest of the ride to Reeses's house was awkwardly silent. Judging from the look on his face, it was obvious his feelings were involved.

When the car came to a stop in front of her door, she wasted no time getting out.

"Damn! Can I at least tell you goodbye?"

"You said that when you pulled in front of my house. I'll call and let you know if I need help with anything."

Frowning, he rolled up his window and smashed off quickly.

Reeses watched until his car made it down the street and then walked smoothly over Beno's house. She moved carefully in her new Giuseppe Zanetti heels while she looked around. Stepping on the porch, she knocked twice.

Beno answered in nothing but some gym shorts and socks. From the looks of his eyes, you could tell he had been woken up from his sleep.

"Reeses? What are you doing up so early?"

"Boy, it's almost eleven o clock. I hope you don't got no little girl running around, 'cause her time is up," she replied, brushing past him.

Beno shook his head as he closed the door and followed her into the bedroom.

Checking the bathroom and closet, Reeses stood in the middle of his floor. Folding her arms, she stared at him seriously.

"Girl, what is your problem?" Beno asked smiling.

"You are. Niggas don't be tired unless they got some pussy around. Now let me find out," she joked, sitting on the bed.

Grabbing a T-shirt out of his closet, he slid it over his head and walked over to the bed to take a seat beside her.

"That was a good one, but you gotta find someone else to play a prank on."

"Mm-hmm. I came to ask you about this product situation. You told me that you needed a new connect to keep the flow going. What have you found?"

Standing up, Beno pulled the large shoebox from under his bed. Lifting the top, he poured the stacks of money on the mattress.

"This is what I've made in the past two days. I don't know what the hell is in it, but I know that we have some top notch quality. My point is, if we find a connect on some cocaine just as good as this, I can make triple times the paper sitting in front of you.

"How much is it?"

"A hundred grand." Beno nodded his head, flipping through a bundle of hundreds.

"Tell me how much you love me," Reeses stated with a huge grin.

"Excuse me?"

Opening her bag, she poured the ten kilos on the top of his bed sheet. "I said tell me how much you love me."

Beno's eyes instantly clicked over to dollar signs when he witnessing all the raw squares. "What the fuck? How in the fuck did you get all of this?"

"That's not important. Do you think we can make the money off it the same?"

Grabbing one, Beno made his way to his dresser. Reeses watched as he cut through the plastic and dipped his pinky, snorting a sample. It didn't take long for the right side of his face to turn numb. Turning around, he paused.

"This shit is damn near the same thing. How are you getting your hands on this?"

"Nigga, just give me my props. I do this hustling shit better than you," Reeses giggled.

Grabbing her into a hug, he spun her around in a circle. "Ahh, I love ya, girl. You gon' be the reason we get rich."

"Put me down, Beno. I'm getting dizzy, boy," Reeses squealed, trying to hold on.

Stopping in place, he planted a soft, passionate kiss on her lips. The fire that shot between her legs caused her to back away.

"I'm sorry," he replied, feeling like he went too far.

"You know how I feel about stuff like that. I told you our friendship is important to me. I don't wanna have to label you a duck like these lames out here. Sit down so we can talk, please."

Walking over to the bed, he took a seat and sat back against the wall.

"Listen, the first time I gave you this stuff, I did it because I really felt bad about your situation. I don't feel you should have to go without if you truly have people in this world who care about you. But now it's business. I want you to be my business partner on this. Everything we make, we split even. I'm telling you this because I wouldn't choose anyone else on something so serious. I'm thinking bigger than a hundred thousand. We could really make a lot of money if I can get you to listen and save the money for us, Beno."

"Listen, Reeses, I know through our life, you haven't seen me accomplish too many things. I've always settled for whatever came my way instead of striving to my fullest potential. I'm gonna keep this shit going by any means necessary. This entire time I've sat here, I waited on a blessing to get my take off. You made that happen and I promise on my life to do right by you.

"I swear if you don't keep your word, I will never forgive you. I need you to really focus on this."

Chapter 9

Slick grunted hard as he entered Natalie from behind. She arched her back and moaned while he roughly stroked inside of her. Placing her fingers over her clit, she twirled them in a circular motion while she looked back at him, taking control. "Fuck this pussy, baby," she cried, feeling herself on the verge of exploding.

Sliding out, Slick buried his face in between her legs, kissing her juices as they flowed down her inner thigh. After tasting her sweet spot for a minute, he rose to his feet, pulling her to the end of the bed.

"Get on your stomach," he demanded, standing in front of her.

Following his orders, she laid on her belly with a huge smile.

Grabbing her by the hair, he placed his rod deeply into her mouth. He began to gag her as she held his waist for support.

"Damn, bitch, you gon' make me lose my fucking mind about you."

Releasing himself on her tongue, he squeezed her ass while she did her normal duties.

"Go hit the shower. I gotta go in here and holla at Blue real quick."

"Alright, baby. I know I got to meet my quota tonight so I might be out till like three," Natalie said, grabbing her a towel.

"Whatever you gotta do to get that paper. I told you, if you ain't worth no paper, it's no point of being around. We gotta pay our way through this life. That's why I keep you around. I know you can make it happen."

After putting on his pants and Nike Air Max, he grabbed his gun and walked out.

It had not even been a full week since Slick had murdered his mother. The paranoia of people talking caused him to lay low for a few days. Everything was right in his face. It was only gonna be a matter of time before he stood with Reeses face to face. It wasn't an option. She would either come off the money or receive a horrible death.

"What the fuck do you niggas got going on?" Slick asked as he got in the living room.

Blue and Quay sat on the couch, passing a giant Dutch master around.

"Open a fucking window. Y'all niggas sitting around kicking shit. What the fuck happened to the vest I asked y'all to get?"

"Relax, big bro. I told you I snatched it up earlier, but you were too busy in Natalie's guts to hear me," Blue said in a drowsy voice.

"Fuck you, bruh. It's money to be made out there in them streets. We ain't got time to be sitting around here getting geeked."

"To be honest, we been waiting on you. We need a re-up. That first batch almost gone. That whipped-ass dope ain't talking 'bout nothing. Why you think it's moving so slow?" Quay said.

"Nah, I didn't know that ass. Of course, I knew the dope is trash. Shit, most of the shit is just baking soda. That's the whole point of the dope game, my nigga. Blue said he's working on the connect fucking with us, so that's straight. Besides, when I set this major move up, we're gonna be beyond up. All you niggas gotta do is pay attention, and by the way, when I crank that li'l play, niggas gotta start pulling up to buy some work. Period."

"Bro, you know we ready. I talked to my people like an hour ago and he said he gon' throw me the birds for nineteen apiece. We got about sixty, so I'll get him to work a deal with me on another note. All you gotta do is take lead my nigga," Blue stated, re-lighting his blunt.

"That's the shit I like to hear. Keep y'all burner too. It's been a lot of shit going on. Clean that basement out like I asked, and I'll call you niggas later," Slick said, walking out the door.

***

It was starting to turn late into the evening, around five o'clock p.m., when Reeses finished counting a hundred grand. After having a portion of the leftover homemade lasagna Beno made the previous night, she stashed her money in the closet and decided to head to the club.

Lately things had started to change. No matter how much she loved the fast money that came from it, being a boss bitch sure wasn't shaking her ass across the stage for a bunch of thirsty-ass niggas all night. The fast money of the drugs kind of excited her. The rush of seeing bundles of thousands knocked anything miscellaneous out of the equation. It was time to quit. Dancing in front of different niggas every day was a downgrade. Her pride was put to the side just for the almighty dollar and that kind of made her feel as if she was being a product of her environment. Only women who showed their hands were the ones who didn't care to expose stand that definitely was a reason to tighten up. You get what you want out of life and Reeses knew that the quick flip was gonna take a boss mind mentality to handle without any distractions. She knew her boss would be extremely mad since she was the star girl of the entertainment spot. A lot of the girls in the club had started to notice her movements and ask too many nosy-ass questions, but opinions were for haters.

Heading out, she jumped in her car and made her way to Magic City. Her energy got live upon hearing Lil Baby's single "My Drip" come through her speakers.

She knew deep down in her heart that quitting the stripping shit was the best idea ever. It was one thing Tasha accomplished with raising her: never take any orders from anyone. Always keep your own, and if you're early, you can never be late to where you're trying to get to. Niggas flaunted unimaginable money in her vision and always pressured her to spoil her with the finest of things. The efforts were wonderful, but only a waste of time. There was nothing that could change Reeses's mind about being the baddest bitch who ever stepped foot into the dope game.

Driving past Garnett Train Station, she made her way to the parking lot of the club. She headed inside and made her way straight to Keith's office. Instead of knocking, she entered to see Rose straddling his lap.

"Goddamn, Reeses. This is still my office. You need to knock," Keith said, embarrassed to be caught with the whore of Atlanta.

"I just need five minutes and then I'm out of your hair."

Rose grabbed her bra from the floor and made her way out the door. Eyeballing Reeses, she closed the door, leaving them to talk.

"Since I haven't seen you in days at the club, I guess you putting in extra hours and coming to tell me where the hell you been," he ranted, sipping his Patron.

"First of all, I'm not coming to tell you shit about where I been and what's going on with me. You aren't even the original owner of this club, sweetie. Just pipe down a little bit," Reeses said calmly.

Keith set down his cup with an awkward look.

"What the hell is wrong with you? Don't come in here with that bad energy shit, Reeses. I'm not the one that got you mad right now. What's the problem?"

"There is no problem. I came to tell you that I'm not coming back. I need to clean out my locker and I also need my money you owe me for the last show I performed."

"What! Are you sick or something? What do you mean you're not coming back to the club?"

"I'm tired of dancing; it's that's simple. I need my payment and I'm going to clean out my space. I've had a wonderful time making this club shine at its highest peak. It's time for me to go," Reeses said, standing up.

Shaking his head, Keith headed to the safe, retrieving the funds. Counting it out, he placed it in her hand and opened his office door. "Good luck!"

"Luck doesn't exist in my world."

Walking out, she headed to the locker room and bagged all her things. Rose sat at her station, getting ready for her private dances.

"Are you leaving?" she asked, looking at Reeses.

"Yes, so go ahead and tell all these other bitches so it won't be any rumors flying. I'm done."

Laughing softly, she walked over to her.

"You think that's something to talk about? I'm ready to get the fuck out of here just like you. Nothing about shaking my ass for a living is cool. I do it because I don't have a choice. You're too young to be in this environment. I'm glad you're making a better choice than me."

Reeses closed her locker, standing face to face with Rose. "Everyone has a choice, and that choice should be whatever benefits you. This ain't it. Hopefully you will try along with all these other girls who are lost."

"I know you're right and I'm not disregarding that. Ever since Dolly came up missing, I've really been thinking about putting this shit on pause."

"What? What do you mean Dolly came up missing?" Reeses said seriously.

"You haven't heard?"

"No, I haven't heard shit. What's going on?"

"Her parents called the club and said they haven't heard from her in a week. She was supposed to meet them on a vacation trip and never made it."

Reeses's heart began to beat fast as she thought hard. "That's not good. How in the fuck has no one seen her? It's something strange going on. I drove by her house a few nights ago and her car was parked there. I knocked, but no one was home."

"Girl, you know like I know that Dolly will go run off for months at a time if she gets the right dick. Remember Tyrese? Or what about the nigga Elay?" She moved to a whole 'nother state. The only thing I don't agree with is her not calling. She wouldn't go without calling us. Now that I kinda think about it, Dolly left to make some money and been gone since."

"I need to get out of here. This is the reason I can't do this. Dolly doesn't want to leave this life because she's too blinded. Keep in contact and let me know what's going on," Reeses mumbled as she left.

"Okay."

Reeses was pissed as she climbed into her car. She had always warned Dolly to be careful with the way she was moving. It was sad to say, but whatever she had going on was on her. Reeses's grandmother's funeral was tomorrow and no negativity was going to throw away her focus on burying her.

Cranking up, she pulled out and headed back to her Smyrna home. Picking up the phone, she called Beno and placed it to her ear.

"Wassup, Rees?"

"Hey, boy. What you doing?" she asked while keeping her eyes on the road.

"I got a little play over here on the eastside. I'ma head that way and handle that. Are you okay?"

"Yeah. I just wanna chill and watch a movie or something. My Nana's funeral is tomorrow and I'm not tryna sit around sad. You know I can't lie to you," she said emotionally.

"Listen, I'll leave my key under the mat. When I finish up in the east, I'll head straight back. I guess I'll cook or something."

"Thank you, Beno."

"You welcome, Rees. I'll see you in a sec," he replied, hanging up.

Chapter 10

Beno got into his new Dodge Challenger straight hellcat. It was all blue with 750 horsepower running through the motor. The 22 Forgiato's placed the finishing touches on the masterpiece. He knew Reeses would think it was too flashy, but that's what money was for. The sad thing about it was that it only cost him twenty zips of cocaine to do it. Niggas would do anything for the rush of pure raw.

Even though Beno was only nineteen, his aptitude for hustling was impeccable. All he needed was the start to take him off. Now, shit was different. Just within in a few days things took a flip and Reeses was the one to thank.

After getting off the phone with her, he dialed his cousin's number.

"Yo, wassup, nigga? Where you at?" the voice answered.

"Nigga, chill yo' happy ass out. I'm heading that way now. Y'all over there in the houses close to Paradise East, right?"

"Yeah, I sent the address earlier. I'm dry as fuck so put a little push in it, bean head-ass nigga!"

Laughing loudly, Beno hung up the phone and turned on the highway.

***

It was around 7:15 when Beno pulled his whip in front of the green one level home. Grabbing the small book bag, he got out and headed to the door.

Blue opened the door with a huge smile.

"Come in, nigga. Ya move like a real turtle, my dude."

"Shut the fuck up," Beno said, stepping into the living room. The red-nosed pit inside the cage by the corner barked loudly as they began to talk.

"That's twenty-five, cuzzo. You know I appreciate you," Blue voiced, putting the money in his hand.

Sliding the loot into his pockets, Beno held up the bag by the strings. "Whole thirty-six. From now on, we gotta do business in the a.m. I'm not really digging the moving at night shit, shawty. As long as it's about the paper, I'm pulling up."

Shaking hands, Blue nodded his head and embraced Beno in a hug.

"I'll be in contact with you in a few days. Just keep the clean coming."

"That's all we got, nigga. And shut that loud-ass dog up. That bitch trippin'," Beno replied, walking onto the porch.

"Man, that's all that bitch do all day, bark. Remember to hit me if you find a link on that gas. That new cat clean as a motherfucker. I like what you doing, nigga. I'm proud of you."

"You know what they say: you can only sit around and wait for so long. It ain't coming to ya. I'll make sure I get at cha if I find something," Beno said, getting in the car.

Blue threw the deuces as Beno backed out of the driveway. He took a seat in the fold out chair.

Slick's Chrysler 300 pulled in slowly. He got out of the car and headed inside.

"Have you heard anything?" he asked, looking at Blue.

"It's sitting on the living room on the table. He just pulled off right before you came. I wish you could have met him real quick. It'll be good for when I'm not around."

"Fuck that, long as you get 'em, we straight. It's a lot of shit going on. I don't need no movement running in and out of my spot. You down for making 20 g's?" Slick asked.

"20 g's? Hell yeah. What the fuck I got to do?"

"Patience. You'll be informed real soon. I'm going to my mother's funeral in the a.m., so stay put. I need you to be here when I get back."

"Bro, I said I got ya."

"Bet. I came to grab a few things and head to Natalie's spot. Make sure you stay on point."

"100!"

Blue dug in his pocket pulling out his box of Newports. After lighting one, he sat back and smiled. Life couldn't be going more perfectly.

***

Getting back to Smyrna, Beno slowed down as he drove down his street. Parking the vehicle, he got out and made his way inside.

Reeses sat on the living room couch, flipping through the channels on the flat screen.

"I see you found something to do," Beno said, taking a seat next to her.

"I didn't have much of a choice. I quit my job at the club today."

A shocked expression formed on his face as he sat up straight. "You did what?"

"I quit."

"I'm proud of you. Real shit. I'm glad you've decided to move away from that stage.

"After my granny's funeral, I'm gonna look into finding an investor about opening up a business or two. It's really a lot of bullshit that I have bundled up. I'm ready to get on my grown woman status. I've had money in my pocket since I was fifteen years old. I've never wanted for shit ever since. I'm thinking for the future now. I wanna hustle after I get enough paper. I wanna leave Georgia and start somewhere else."

"You really serious about this hustling thing, huh?" Beno asked, feeling her idea.

"I'm beyond serious. I want to stamp my name as the queen of this. I'm not meeting with people if it isn't necessary. It's all a game. If we move correct, we can beat the odds and make it out with everything."

"I'm with it. Whatever step you take, I promise to stand with you and do this. Downs and ups," Beno said, placing his hand on her right knee.

"I believe you."

Looking into his eyes, he dropped his head, trying to choose his next words carefully.

"I know all our time we've known each other, I've always told you I cared, that I would always be there for you and be a true friend, Reeses. I can't spend my life without you. Even when I sleep, I think about you. I can't handle anything happening to you. I've always wanted a chance to prove that I truly love you," he said, speaking his heart.

A light tear formed in her eyes upon hearing his gentle words. "Beno, out of all these girls you can probably get at, why me? Why do you love me so much?"

"Because I know in my heart no one will fight to the end of the earth for you as I will. Since sixth grade, I followed you around like a puppet. Years later I'm still here, and my heart still hasn't changed. I still worship the ground you walk on. I've spent six years being the most loyal friend to you. Now I wanna live in the first six years of making you my queen."

No matter what doubt she put in her mind, she knew he was right. She never could shake him. The attraction was always there, but never presented. The friendship they shared was irreplaceable. The only thing that scared her was the almighty power of love.

She paused to speak, but was cut off from Beno's lips kissing her slowly. His tongue roamed the inside of her mouth, taking her breath away.

"Reeses, I love you, but I don't think I can let you be with another man. I refuse to let you slip away from me."

"Please, Beno, just let me think," she whispered, feeling the fire in between her legs.

Standing up, he shed his clothes and stood in front of her butt naked. "Think about it while I make love to you."

Reeses gasped upon seeing the size of his manhood. Her words were stuck as he reached for her pants and pulled them gently off her waist and let them fall to the floor. Picking her up around his waist, he walked her into the bedroom, staring at her with a deep passion.

Placing her on the bed, he pulled off her black lace panties. Her skin was crawling with bubbles as she held her mouth open, speechless.

Beno kissed her lips and headed straight for dessert. Twirling his tongue around her clit, he sucked heavily, tasting her sweetness. His head slid up and down her kitten, licking her softly.

"Beno, wait!" Reeses moaned, not knowing what she was feeling.

He ignored her, burying his face deeper with every movement. Taking his time, he kissed over her body gently, getting every spot. He couldn't help but be pleased, seeing her eyes roll slowly as her perfect body shone to perfection.

Raising up, his rod stood at attention in front of him. Moving his body slowly on top of hers, he kissed her neck and lips, trying to enter her.

"Beno, wait, you're gonna hurt me!" Reeses cried with a scared look.

"I'm not gonna hurt you, baby. I told you, I love you."

"Beno, I'm a virgin."

Taking a deep breath, he paused. "Are you serious?"

"Yes."

Wiping her tears away, he kissed her lips. "I promise I won't hurt you. Wrap your arms around my neck."

Mounting her, he placed the head of his manhood inside her slowly. Flinching from the feeling of his size, Reeses held onto his neck tighter. Her grey eyes sparkled in euphoria as Beno lightly penetrated her. Sliding out of her, she watched while he eased into her wet pussy deeply.

"Ahh fuckkk," she moaned, feeling her vision blurring.

The rough sensational feeling ceased when he popped her innocence out of her system. Her sweet spot began to flow quickly while Beno filled her small pussy.

"Damn, you feel so good, Reeses."

His passionate strokes began to turn into long, slow ones. As he gripped her waist, her heart skipped a beat and she felt the powerful clenching inside of her stomach. She instantly dropped a tear as her first orgasm erupted. Pulling at the sheets, she gasped.

His dick pumped back and forth. He spread her legs further apart, allowing it to fill her completely.

"Beno! What are you doing to me?" Reeses panted, feeling dizzy.

"I'm making love to you. I'm making you mines," he spoke with ease, keeping his stroke just right.

Gripping her breasts, he rubbed and touched all her spots the right way. His gentle fingers sliding across her stomach caused her to cum on his love stick for a second time.

"Please, Beno, stop," Reeses whispered, feeling her heart beat extremely hard.

Releasing inside of her, he rolled over, pulling her close to him. She closed her eyes, trying to stop the room from spinning. Catching her breath, she opened them and grabbed ahold of his hand.

"I warned you not to do this to me. I really hope and pray that your intentions are real for me. I love you, Beno," she said, passing out on his chest.

Listening to her words, he gripped her tightly, kissing her forehead.

"I promise on my soul that I will never hurt you. I will always cherish you, Reeses. I love you too."

She didn't respond, but his voice rang inside of her. To everyone else, Beno might have been a lame or coward. In her eyes, he was loyal and much more.

Wrapping her leg around him, she thought about what the future held. No matter what, she was positive about her new profession. Money was meant to be made by any means.

Chapter 11
Westview Cemetery (10:45 a.m.)

The rain poured lightly as Reeses rose out of her seat and placed the rose on her grandmother's casket. Her tears poured down her face as she said a silent prayer. She sat back down and the preacher said his final words, ending the ceremony for a woman who would be remembered forever.

Looking at her side, her facial expression went from sad to pure anger.

"Hey Reeses. How are you?" Slick asked, walking up to her.

He still looked the same way as he did ten years ago. The ache and hurt he caused to her mother ran through her head. The grimy look showed clearly in his eyes.

"What the fuck do you want?" she asked, standing to her feet and taking a step back.

"Is that how you treat ya uncle? We need to talk. I know it's been a lot going on."

"You're not my fucking uncle and we don't have a bitch-ass thing to talk about."

"I think we do, silly-ass li'l girl. My mother is dead, and she didn't even have nothing to take to her grave with her. You got all that paper and my fucking mama laid up sick with all those medical bills piled to the roof. You owe her. That's a whole lot to talk about right there," Slick said a little more aggressively.

"Fuck you! I don't owe you shit. You didn't love my nana and you're a fucking slime ball. I'm warning you, stay the fuck away from me or else!"

"Is that a threat, bitch?"

"Is there a problem here? Are you two alright?" the pastor asked, stepping near them.

"We're fine. I was just leaving," Reeses said, making her way through the small field of grass.

Slick chuckled lightly, watching her get into the car and leave.

"God bless you, sir," Slick said to the pastor, walking off.

***

The rage that Reeses felt in her heart was unthinkable. The destruction Slick caused when she was a child continuously flipped through her brain as she pulled inside the small car dealership.

Seeing the reasonable prices up for grabs, she parked and headed inside. A few car salesmen moved about, helping potential buyers. Her antennas raised upon seeing the tall man dressed in a blue suit sitting behind the counter.

"Excuse me. Is there any way I can speak to the manager?"

Standing up, he smiled and held his hand out. "That would be me. My name is Earnest Medial. How can I help you?"

"I'm looking for a car. Nothing too flashy, but nothing old either. I need something plain and up to date."

"Ma'am, this is Pro Auto's. We distribute a different variety of custom cars. I'm positive we can find something you will like. Are you looking to lease?"

"No. I wanna buy it. Cash."

Looking at her with a stern expression, he cleared his throat. "Every car out there is over twenty thousand dollars. If you truly wished to pay in cash, we will need statements and proof of this currency to validate inside our system. Do you know anything about your credit score?"

"Look, I'm gonna just be honest. I would like to skip past the whole paper procedure thing and just keep this under the table. If it's a yes, I will deposit ten grand now and sign the papers tomorrow. I can have the other half to you around noon."

Adjusting his tie, he licked his lips, looking into Reeses's grey eyes.

"I can pull a few strings if I can get the chance to take you out with me. I know a good Mexican restaurant if you like to eat," he replied, sounding extra fucking corny.

Flashing a bright smile, Reeses shook her head. "You don't even know my name. Don't let me find out you be riding with a whole bunch of strangers. I'm also still waiting on your answer about this lucky business question."

"Oh, yeah, of course. I have something in mind I know would fit you. It's gonna run you twenty-two even. Hold your funds and we can meet in the a.m. to handle the paperwork."

"Well, thank you for your time and I guess I'll see you tomorrow."

Straightening his collar, he looked around to see who was observing. "Damn!" he grumbled to himself, watching Reeses's ass rock from side to side as she left.

Getting back out to her car, she thought hard on her plan. Switching up cars would stop a lot of people from pointing her out. People tend to keep their eyes on shit that you allow them to watch, so slipping up was out of the question. The only thing left was to look for a relocation spot. It was never too safe to keep a duck off that's secluded to the outsiders.

Hearing the loud thunder that erupted in the sky caused her to jump. The grey clouds began to form quickly in the air. Her mind was so distracted, she hadn't realized it was raining.

"Shit!" Reeses uttered, turning on her windshield wipers.

Looking down at her phone, she viewed the missed call from the federal institution. Calling Beno's phone, she received no answer and placed it inside her pocket.

After a rough ten minute drive, the rain began to fall harder as she exited the expressway. Thinking about her hair, she knew that the day couldn't get any worse.

Heading down her street, she parked in front of her house and got out. Trying her best not to slip, she moved carefully in the red bottom heels to the door. After finding her key, she walked in quickly, shaking the rain from her purse and hand.

The sight of her destroyed home paused her movements. The first thought that came to her mind was the cash stashed inside of her closet. Running through the hallway, she slammed her purse down after seeing her room door caved in.

"Damn it!" Reeses yelled, walking through the mess that covered the floor.

The ringtone from her cell sounded off. Pulling it out of her pocket, she answered without looking.

"Hello?"

The loud cries that poured through the line made it hard for her to hear.

"Reeses, where are you?"

"Who is this?"

"It's Rose. Reeses, you need to get over here to Dolly's house now." She cried heavily.

"Rose, calm down. Tell me what's going on."

"They found Dolly dead inside of her trunk. The entire street is surrounded."

Reeses's heart stopped upon hearing Rose's words. "Oh my God! I'm on the way now."

When she checked her closet and saw all the empty shoeboxes scattered inside, she knew that her luck was over. The cash was gone and whoever had it took every dime. Standing up, she made her way quickly to the front door

As her foot stepped past the corner of the living room, the fist that collided with her temple knocked her out instantly.

"Shit, for a bitch who talks a lot of shit, I woulda thought you can take a punch," Slick said, standing over her body. Pulling out his flip phone, he dialed a number, waiting for an answer.

"Yeah?"

"Pull around with the car. I got her."

Hanging up the line, he placed a zip tie around Reeses's hands and feet. Hearing the phone vibrate in his pocket, he opened the front door.

The rain continued to spill hard while he made his way back to Reeses and picked her up.

Walking outside, he walked through the storm, watching the water dance across her face.

Quay opened the back door of the car, allowing Slick to put her on the seat. Climbing in beside her, he placed a brown bag over her head and shut the door.

***

Two hours later

Beno drove slowly down the street with a huge smile on his face. He knew for a fact that Reeses would be happy with the new four bedroom home he found for her. It was nice and in the perfect area. The price was reasonable, so he took it upon himself to put down the first payment. If his calculations were on point, the house would be paid off within three months. All he had to do was keep the product bumping and the rest would fall into play. It was awkward how you could go years loving your best friend and then have things turn out exactly how you dreamed. He smiled, thinking of the day he could make her his wife.

Parking his car behind Reeses's, he grabbed his dead cell phone out of the cup holder and got out.

Walking towards the house, he raised his eyebrow, looking at her open front door. Stepping inside, his mouth opened wide as he looked around quickly. The living room looked as if someone sent a tornado flying straight through it. Looking at the flipped furniture and the broken glass, he knew something was terribly wrong

"Reeses?" he yelled out with his heart thumping harder than a bass drum.

He creeped around every corner, checked every room, and made his way back to the front of the house. Quickly reaching in his back pocket, he fumbled with his phone, trying to turn it on.

"What in the fuck is going on?" he mumbled to himself, trying to call her number before the dead battery cut the line off.

He began to wonder harder after he didn't receive an answer from the four calls he placed to her phone. Looking down at the small dots of blood on the carpet, he did the only thing he could. He dialed 911.

***

Not even ten minutes later, over nine cop cars had the entire street locked. Beno sat on the hood of his car, tapping his feet, waiting patiently. The crime scene unit went about dusting for prints and scanning the home for any clue.

Beno stood off the hood of the Challenger as an officer approached him.

"Sir, when is the last time you heard from this woman?"

"I told you the first time, I haven't seen her since last night. She was supposed to attend her grandmother's funeral this morning. That's all I know."

"Hey, listen, asshole. I'm just trying to figure out what happened here. Now you need to watch your fucking mouth because if you ask me, buddy, you're starting to be suspect number 1."

"Are you fucking kidding me? While you're sitting here wasting time, she could be fucking dead! Snap out of the racist Uncle Tom act and do your fucking job!" Beno yelled.

Spotting the altercation, a few detectives made their way over, posting silently. Placing his hand on top of his weapon, the officer stepped closer to Beno.

"This is my last time telling you this. Calm the fuck down or I'll arrest you right now for obstruction. Let us do our fucking job. When we find out anything, we will contact you. This is no longer your business. I need you to exit this scene and let the authorities do what they are paid for," the man ranted with a card between his fingers.

Rubbing the side of his temples, Beno grabbed the card and stormed off towards his car. It was obvious the police didn't care for the situation as he did. Cranking his engine, he sped off to find the answers to his questions.

***

Reeses's heart thumped fast upon hearing the voices around her. The small lamp that sat across from her shone brightly, blocking her vision when Slick pulled the bag from her head.

"Good morning, niecey pooh. I thought you would never wake up," he slurred with an evil smile.

His clothes reeked of marijuana and from the looks of his red eyes, he was probably on a few other things as well. Her facial expression tightened and she tried to slide up against the wall with her back.

"Awww! What's wrong? You're not happy to see me? All that gangsta-ass shit you was talking earlier. You must didn't really mean that, huh?" Slick asked, rubbing through her hair.

"I haven't done nothing to you. Why am I here?" Reeses shook in fear.

"Jimmie, Jimmie, punk-ass Jimmie. You look just like that bitch-ass nigga. While I spent my days taking care of my mother, she praised a motherfucker who wasn't even her blood son. Can you believe it? This nigga comes into my mom's home and takes my role like I was never even born. I mean, she would literally give her soul for this man," Slick said, looking at Quay with a psychotic smile.

Reeses stared at him quietly, hearing the hate spit from his tongue.

"A little birdie told me my brother ran across a mean-ass payday a while back. I asked for help. I asked him to lend a hand. He didn't. I need you to listen closely. I need that money and I know you have it. Don't make me kill you for it, please!"

"I don't know what you're talking about," she whimpered with tears in her eyes.

Pulling out his phone, he stepped closer to her, bending down.

"This is what I'm gonna do. I'll give you one call to tell whoever you can to bring the money before I kill you. If you mention my name, I'll blow your brains out with no hesitation. This is the first warning before I get impatient."

As she looked at the phone, Fresh instantly ran through her head. She knew that Slick was serious. Fresh was the only person she knew really in the streets to handle a fuck nigga like Slick accordingly.

"404-555-9966," she mumbled, hoping he would answer. Dialing the numbers into the pad, he placed the phone on speaker, holding it towards her. Reeses listened to the line ring, feeling the chills claw at her skin.

"Yo, who dis?"

"Fresh, please help me. I need you to listen to me."

"Reeses? Man, what the fuck do you want? You got you a li'l work. You shouldn't need help with anything."

"Fresh, I'm in trouble!"

Snatching the phone back, Slick placed it towards his mouth.

"Aye, listen up, my nigga. I don't know who you are to this little cunt, but she owes me a lot of paper. 1.9 million, to be exact. If you have any love for her, I suggest you gather that or she won't be able to make another call unless it's to heaven."

"Who the fuck is dis? Nigga, do you know who the fuck you talking to? Fuck you and that bitch. I ain't coming off shit for that bitch. She ain't my hoe. So whatever type of game y'all playing, you need to find the right nigga to try it with," he replied, hanging up.

"Mmm, mmm, mmm, looks like you in a little bit of trouble, Rinesha. It seems to me that your companion has left you on stuck. How do you propose we handle this?"

Reeses continued to look at him quietly in fear as Beno crossed her mind.

"Can I make another call?"

Slick smiled, placing the phone in his back pocket.

"Unfortunately, that's not gonna happen. Too many calls alerts too many people and I'm not for the whole chasing game. Tell me where the fuck the money is, and we can end this."

"I don't have any money," she shouted with tears in her eyes.

"Bitches are so stupid. Sometimes you all have to learn the hard way. I'm going to find it one way or the other and when I do, you're gonna wish you were never born."

Rubbing his hands together, he looked over at his loyal worker.

"Quay, hand me the curling irons."

Chapter 12

It had been over three hours since Beno left the authorities and there still wasn't any sign of Reeses. His mind couldn't function. He knew in his soul something terrible was wrong.

Driving past the small Wayfield Plaza, he spotted his old co-worker Shaun posted in front of the building. Clicking his blinker, he made a left turn into the lot and pulled down in front of him.

"Beno?" Shaun said, looking surprised.

"What's good, bro? Let me holla at you for a second."

"Nigga, what the fuck happened? Did you hit the lottery or some shit? When did you get the new hell cat?" he asked, rubbing the side of the car.

"I've had it for a while. I need to ask you something," Beno replied seriously.

"Wassup, my dude?"

"Have you seen Reeses slide past through here today?"

"Nah, I haven't. Did you hear the word going around the neighborhood?" Shaun asked, moving his head closer to the window of the car.

Beno raised his eyebrows with a weird facial expression. "What the fuck are you talking about?"

"The nigga Fresh rolled through earlier today stressing some shit 'bout she was kidnapped or something. He looked like he was mad as fuck, cuz. All he kept stressing was her cutting in on his paper or some shit. He tried to sell my brother some weight, but the shit was cut like a motherfucker, so he just left," Shaun said, busting down his White Owl cigar.

"Hold the fuck up! What? Who the hell is Fresh? Where did he hear this shit from?"

"Fresh, man. The nigga who been supplying the little weight that's floating around. He used to pull up to the plaza in the all-black Cadillac truck a while back and drop my shit off to me. Remember?"

"Where the fuck is he?" Beno asked with fire dancing in his pupils.

Shaun could tell from the sound of his voice that the news wasn't sitting well with him.

"Hey, look, bro, I know Reeses supposed to be your little friend or whatever, but I'm telling you this because I fuck with you. Don't go playing with that man. He don't fuck around and I don't wanna see you getting hurt. From what I understand, Reeses and Fresh been fucking with each other."

"I said where can I find him?" Beno asked more aggressively.

Shaking his head, Shaun lit his blunt and stepped back. "You about to get mixed in with some gangsta shit and end up getting killed. The suburb town homes that sit down in Powder Springs. Just look for the truck. Don't get me tied up in this shit if something happens," he voiced with a pathetic face, walking off.

Beno let Shaun's words soak in before he slowly pulled off. He didn't know if what he spoke was the truth. The entire situation was starting to jumble up his thoughts. Reeses would never have anything going on without him knowing about it, especially when it came to dealing with a man. There was something terribly wrong going on and no answers except the one Shaun had just given him. There was only one way to find out. There was no other option.

***

"Fuck you!" Reeses grunted shaking from the heated irons pressed against her right thigh.

Quay posted in the corner, covering his ears from her loud yelling. The smell of her flesh burning reamed the room while Slick pressed the metal down harder. Wiping the sweat from his face, he stood up straight and began to laugh. "You really do not know how fucked up my mind is when it comes to this shit. If you weren't my niece, I would probably have my dick stuffed inside your mouth. Can you go ahead and tell me where my paper is at so this can be over?" he asked, taking a swig of the Patron bottle.

Reeses face cringed, trying to subdue the pain that was running inside her body. She held eye contact with him as he maneuvered back and forth in front of her.

"I don't have any fucking money! Everything I had was inside of my closet. There's nothing left, Slick," she pleaded, not trying to give in.

"How did I know you were going to say something like that? I guess sometimes you gotta put in a little extra work to make a lot of shit happen."

Grabbing his gun off the small table, he checked his chamber and slid it behind his back. Walking back towards her, he grabbed the back of her head and stared into the eyes of his brother's daughter.

"Tell ya what. I'm gonna make a little trip back to your house and search a little more thoroughly and while I'm at it, I'll make a detour on the way back to my mother's house. I'm gonna find that money, and if I really have to go through all of this to get it in my hands, I'm gonna put two bullets inside of your head and dump yo' stupid ass inside Lake Lanier!" he yelled, releasing her hair.

Making his way up the basement steps, he stopped and looked over at Quay.

"Keep an eye on that bitch! If she do something stupid, beat the fuck out of her. After I get this money, we can kill her," Slick grumbled before walking out.

Quay grinned, looking over at Reeses in her black form-fitting dress.

"Now if you can keep a secret, I will," he said, moving towards her slowly.

Her eyes burned with hatred as he placed his hand on her thigh, rubbing against the fresh burns she had just received. Her chest heaved and she tensed from the shocking pain. Quay trailed his fingers up her leg and eased her dress up, exposing her perfect print through the black lace panties she wore.

The ringing of his cell phone stopped him, causing him to dig in his pocket.

"Nigga, what the fuck you want?" he answered quickly, seeing the name that was on the cell.

"Nigga, fuck you! Are you at the spot or not?" Blue asked, inhaling on the new moon rock weed he had just purchased.

"Of course, nigga. My mind stays focused on money. Where the fuck are you?"

"Standing in front of the house, ass wipe. Come open the door so we can smoke this gas, silly-ass li'l boy."

"I'm on my way up," Quay replied, smiling down into Reeses's face.

Pressing the end button, he caressed her face and blew her a kiss.

"Looks like we gotta get together a little later, love bug. The weed's calling my name."

Running up the steps, he opened the door and left.

The loud dog that began to bark, echoed through the upstairs floor as Reeses listened for anything she could hear. She wiggled her hands in the zip ties, but the strong plastic only gave her so much room to move. Her tears began to lightly drip down her cheeks while she prayed for an escape from this horrible nightmare.

***

Ten hours later

Beno sat on the couch in his living room as the rage grew in his body. His heart began to thump slower and he gripped his fingers tightly together. Reeses's face flashed through his mind, making his skin crawl with anger and sadness mixed together.

Looking down at the small pile of cocaine he had left on his table from earlier, he bent his head down and snorted a huge line. He quickly threw his head back, feeling the rush of the drug hit his nostrils. Clutching his fist tightly, he grabbed the lamp, slamming it across the wall. His emotions began to spill over as he stood up and headed towards his bedroom. Cutting on his light, he moved over to his mattress and flipped it over.

He picked up the black M-16 assault rifle, grabbed the fully loaded magazine, and inserted it inside the bottom. Grabbing his black duffle bag, he placed it in and picked up his two Glocks. Placing them on his hip, he grabbed his leather coat and skull cap before leaving out of the crib.

Opening the trunk, he tossed the duffle bag in and climbed into the driver seat.

If God was real, Beno prayed that he watched over whoever was involved with the pain that was knocking through his chest.

Chapter 13
Atlanta, Georgia - Federal Institution

The gate to the federal penitentiary slid open slowly when the guard officer pressed the button. He eyed Jack as he walked out into the open lot. Spotting his brother standing posted twenty feet away, he made his way in front of him.

"I thought they was never gon' let you out of that muthafucka," Poker spoke, flicking down the end of his Newport.

"How long have you been out here?"

"They let me out about thirty minutes ago. The taxi been out here about ten minutes waiting on us. It's good to see you, bro, but how are we gonna handle this situation?"

"I knew something was wrong. I tried calling for her the past couple of days and still couldn't reach her. We pulling up on everybody until I find her. All of them niggas!" Justin said with a straight face.

"My people told me the spot is ready. We can head there, then it's all up to you. I want her back just as bad as you do," Phil whispered, lighting another smoke.

Justin frowned and the anger was imprinted on his expression. He simply nodded his head while they headed towards the parked white taxi.

"Just to let you know before this shit starts, I'm not holding back," Phil voiced before they climbed in and pulled away.

"Where to, fellas?" the white man asked, looking through his rearview mirror at the two identical men in his back seat.

"Take us to Laurel Ridge Apartments off Camp Creek," Phil replied in a humble tone.

***

Beno slowly pulled his Challenger in front of the all-white town home. Placing the car in park, he left the engine running and exited the driver side after spotting the all-black Cadillac truck parked inside the space.

He pulled his skull cap down lower over his face as he looked around at his surroundings. Stepping up on the porch deck, he knocked three times and waited patiently.

Fresh opened the door, looking into Beno's cold eyes.

"Nigga, who the fuck are you? You might got the wrong house."

"I'm looking for Reeses."

"What! Nigga, who the fuck you supposed to be?" Fresh asked, screwing up his face.

Beno pulled his gun quickly from his hip and placed it inside Fresh's mouth. Pushing him backwards in the house, he kicked the door closed.

"Yo! Yo! Yo! Hold up! Hold up! What's going on, bro?" Fresh panicked out of fear of being shot.

"Where in the fuck is my girl?"

The cold steel that rested on Fresh's forehead caused his bowels to release in his pants. "I don't know shit, nigga. That's on my mama's soul!"

Boc! The gun released sending a bullet through his foot.

"Agh! Arghhh! Okay! Okay!"

"Shut the fuck up! Tell me what the fuck I want to know!" Beno demanded in rage.

"It had to be her manager at Magic City, bruh. The nigga's slime. I was with him the other day and he was ranting and furious about her quitting the club. I hadn't seen her in a few days and she called my phone saying she was in trouble. Don't kill me, my nigga." Fresh sweated heavily, in pain.

"What's his name?"

"Everybody calls him Keith. He's there every night. I swear to you. I ain't got none to do with that li'l bitch going missing."

Pressing the gun into Fresh's stomach forcefully, Beno pulled the trigger three times, letting him crash to the floor.

Moving past him, he began to look through the house from top and bottom. His actions were pointless because he still didn't find Reeses. Running the recent info he had just been given back in his head, he stepped back over Fresh's dead body and calmly walked out of the home with a black cloud that rained directly on top of him.

***

Laurel Ridge Apartments

Standing in the bathroom mirror, Justin picked up his prayer rug from the floor and folded it into a neat square. Even after ten years in the feds, he had come home to a disaster. Reeses was the only peace of sanity he held onto besides Allah. Losing their mom was even harder, not to mention Jimmie was gone too.

Exiting the bathroom, he walked into the living room, where Phil stood with a half empty glass of tequila.

"It feels weird having ya back right here. I literally ain't seen you in ten years and we been in the same penitentiary."

"A few weeks after our trial, I paid our attorney to get with the judge about us serving our time in state for the sake of Mom and Reeses. We were all they had left. It didn't work so well because they blocked all connections with me and you while we served our time."

"Yeah, I know. While she broke her neck to get in contact with you, I sat back, paving out my own way to keep in tune with these streets. My people put this little crib right here together a few months back before our release. We got everything we need: clothes, straps, and food."

"Bro, I know you've been through a lot since we've been gone. Allah is my witness that I didn't, nor did our sister, shut you out."

"When did the fuck you turn into a Jew?" Phil replied, chuckling.

"I'm a Muslim, li'l bro. And Allah was the best thing that happened to me. I found the way for us, and if we pay attention to it, we will prosper and get our sister back first."

Smacking his teeth, Phil lit the cigarette that sat behind his ear. "Whatever! How are we about to handle this shit we got going on now?"

"Somebody gon' tell us something. That's for damn sure. I just don't need us going back to prison before we get to make sure that our sister is alive."

"You know just like I know who's first on my fucking suspect list. We've been gone ten years, Justin. Our sister has gotten older, not to mention she's stripping. Our friends have been trying to fuck our little sister since we've been gone. It's no other links to her, period. Everyone else is dead."

"I just don't want any innocent people getting hurt."

"Look, I say we push up on all these niggas' asses one by one. If they play, we dust they asses and keep moving until that lucky bird sings. I guarantee we will find her."

"I pray to Allah that we do."

The streets had flipped hundreds of times since the twins had been locked away. A lot of people had questions to answer or hell was about to be brought to everyone that made the list.

***

Slick cracked his eyes, lifting Natalie's arm off his waist, and stood from the bed. He had spent his entire night running around looking for the stash that was rightfully owed to him. Grabbing his phone, he began to check for any missed calls while he searched for a set of clean clothes.

Natalie sat up in the bed and placed her back against the back board, folding her arms. She mugged Slick. "I hope you know if you leave out after you just told me you are staying two days, don't come back."

"Baby, shut up. You know this money gotta be made. I just told you by next week I should be able to buy you a boat or some shit."

"Nigga, I don't want no fucking boat. I want you to start staying your ass at home. I'm tired of coming to fuck you inside of a trap spot."

"I told you why we move the way we do, silly-ass girl. It's hot right now and I'm not about to take any falls for nobody, not even myself. All you gotta do is count this money and think about where the fuck we about to have our honeymoon."

Flashing a bright smile, Natalie wrapped her arms around his neck, kissing his lips. "I hear ya, daddy. You still need to remember that family is important, though. Don't let money destroy our relationship. It's not about how much we got. The love builds up the missing pieces."

As she made her way to the bathroom, Slick pondered her words. In his brain, all that shit was just a myth. Paper controlled everything. Without money, you didn't have a life. Thinking about the payday that was ahead, his thirst grew larger.

He had waited ten years, but time was finally up. One way or another, he knew it would be found. It was only a matter of time.

Dialing a number into his cell, he placed it to his ear.

"Yo, wassup, big bro?" Shaun asked through the line.

"What's good, li'l homie? You ready for me to come and pick that li'l paper up?"

"Yeah! I was about to go post up at the plaza in a second, but I overslept."

"Nigga, ain't nobody standing on the corner no more. You got a car, my boy. I suggest you use it."

"You know what they say, big bro. If you by yourself, the only person that can tell on you, is you. I'll be up there at the Wayfield in about twenty minutes."

"I'll be there," Slick replied before hanging up.

***

Blue fired up the Garcia Vega full of kush while he maneuvered around Quay, who lay asleep on the floor.

"Man, nigga, where in the fuck are the Newports?"

"They in the deep freezer in the basement, nigga. Leave me the fuck alone," Quay grumbled, placing the cover over his head.

"What type of motherfuckers keep the cigarettes in the damn freezer?" Shaking his head, he inhaled on the blunt as he made his way through the basement door. Taking the steps two at a time, he walked over to the freezer that sat straight ahead. After grabbing the fresh carton of smokes, he lightly jumped upon seeing Reeses sitting in the corner with hurt written over her face. Her eyes stayed glued to him while she twisted her wrists back and forth from the irritating plastic.

"What the fuck?"

The desperate look alerted him that something very wrong was going on. Her grey eyes begged him to come release her and from the looks of her chest heaving up and down heavily, you could tell she was scared.

Quickly heading back upstairs, he walked over to Quay, nudging him.

"Bruh, what the fuck is going on around here?" Blue asked with a serious expression.

"Man, what the fuck are you talking about, and why are you waking me the fuck up? Niggas get shot for that in certain hoods, bruh!"

"Fuck all that! It's a bitch tied up in the basement downstairs. Did you know that?"

Standing up, Quay grabbed the smokes out of his hand and opened them. Placing one in his mouth, he grabbed the lighter off the table and sparked it.

"Of course I knew that, dumb ass. Why in the fuck do you think I'm still here? It's not gonna be for long though. After the business is handled, we will get rid of her."

"What the fuck do mean get rid of her? That's somebody's daughter. That shit gon' make the spot hot!" Blue said, thinking smart.

"Nigga, Slick got everything under control. We about to be up twenty racks after this. All you gotta do is sit back and let me handle the rest."

"Well try to start letting me know before your niggas start taking bitches off the street innocently. I told my people to pull up over here. I don't need him getting nervous about some small shit."

"I said I got the bitch," Quay replied loudly, causing the dog to bark.

Feeling his phone vibrate, Blue looked down at Beno's number and picked up.

"I'm here."

"You coming out now?"

Opening the front door, Blue grabbed the small book bag sitting by the entrance and walked out.

***

Beno pulled his car over in the front of his cousin's work spot. Even though the paper was a must, his mind wandered to the next person in line for questioning. Reeses was the only thing sitting in his mind. He prayed in his heart that God could keep her safe because his journey wouldn't stop until he found her.

Stepping out of his car, he walked towards the front steps where Blue stood.

"Wassup, cuzzo? I see you still kicking good shit."

Beno flashed a fake smile, handing him the brown paper bag.

"You a'ight, bro?" Blue asked, handing him the bag of cash.

"Yeah, I'm good. I just got a lot of shit going on. I'll be fine."

"Nigga, you my cousin. You know if you got a problem, I'm here. Did a nigga try you or some?" Blue questioned, screwing up his face.

"Nah, bro! I told you I'm good. If I need you, I'll call," Beno said, heading back towards the car.

"Cool. I'm here if you need me."

Climbing in the driver seat, Beno cranked the car and pulled off. He refused to involve anyone, especially his family, with the terrible situation that was at hand. In his eyes, no one cared for Reeses the way he did, and that one statement would be known through the entire city until he took his last breath.

Chapter 14
Cobble Stone Apartments

It was around four in the afternoon when Phil finally spotted Cadarius walking around the corner. From the look of his glistening chain and watch, you could tell he had been eating over the past ten years instead of sitting around. The twins sat patiently, watching him serve the constant traffic that moved through the building. You could tell he was comfortable from the wads of cash that consumed his pockets and the small handheld gun that dangled on his waist.

"Are you ready or what?" Phil asked, itching to show his face to the streets again.

"Yeah, I am, but I don't want any reflexive plan bouncing back in our face. I'm trying to keep us on a low key level."

"Well, show me how it's done, and I'll follow."

Fixing the handle of the gun on his waistline, he stepped out of the car and placed on his kufi.

The crowds had begun to disperse while Cadarius sat on the curb, counting the quick cash he recently made.

"Say, Cadarius. I need to holla at you for a minute."

Looking up from where he sat, his face started to turn a shade lighter, looking into Justin's eyes.

"Jack? What the fuck? When did you get out?" he replied, placing the money back in his pants quickly.

"That's not important. I need to ask you a few questions about my sister."

Spotting the handle of Justin's gun, he jolted into action, running across the grass towards the back parking lot.

Phil spotted the movements and mashed the pedal down full force. The engine of the car roared, speeding around the side corner of the building.

Cadarius held on to his falling pants, running as fast as he could. The car approaching caused his heart to race and he realized he was blocked in.

Before he could make any sudden moves, Phil jumped out of the car with his pistol aimed with two hands.

"Don't even think about reaching for that shit, Darius!"

Justin appeared from around the corner with his gun in hand as if everything was normal. Walking over to Cadarius, he looked him sternly in the eyes before he spoke. "If you have anything to do with this, you need to let us know now."

"Jack, this is me you talking to. I wouldn't play with you or Poker like that. I don't have nothing to do with her being taken."

"We never told you she was taken, dumb ass. Come up with the next lie," Phil said aggressively.

"Can you tell us anything that will lead us in the right direction, Cadarius? This is not meant for you. We need to find out what happened to our sister."

"You niggas been gone for ten years, bro. Shit is different. If I tell you anything, I'ma die. I ain't going out bad," he replied, reaching for the 9mm gun inside his pocket.

Bloc! Bloc! Bloc! Bloc! Bloc!

Justin stood in silence as he watched Phil gun down a man they once knew as a friend.

Jumping back inside the car, Justin mugged Phil as he pulled back around front swerving out of the apartments.

"What?"

"Why in da fuck did you shoot him, bro? He didn't know anything."

"Nah, you got shit confused. He didn't kidnap her, but he knew something. I could tell by how nervous he was, and plus the motherfucker reached for his strap. I ain't letting a nigga down bad us, period," Phil boasted, bending the next few turns smoothly.

Justin kept his eyes on the view behind them, shaking his head.

"You need to start relegating your thinking and form a new approach, li'l bro. If we don't move a little more silent, we will be back in prison within the next few days."

"I'm not going back to prison. I can promise you that. I'd rather be carried by six than judged by twelve. We either gonna find our sister or we not. Are you in or out?"

Holding his tongue, Justin sat back in the seat, viewing the streets from the passenger window. They hadn't even felt the Atlanta weather for a full day and a man's blood was on their hand. He hoped and prayed differently, but knew things were about to get worse.

***

Detective Berkley swiftly moved through the precinct building, past the rookie officers to the Captain's office. Knocking quickly, he entered before he could get a reply.

"Captain Myers, do you have a quick second, sir?" he asked, taking a seat and opening the file up.

"I know you aren't taking no for an answer anyway. Shoot your shot," he replied, taking his attention from the laptop in front of him.

"You know there is still an active case about the missing person report on the break in."

"This is the report about the young girl. I'm still aware, and we still have an active unit out on the search. We're tracing all of her recent contacts and still in search of the family members."

"That's my problem, sir. I did a little research on her myself. Did you know that this is Jimmie Rivers's daughter?" Detective Berkley asked, sliding a picture of the mugshot across his desk.

Picking up the lineup photo, Captain Myers placed on his glasses and stared at the man who caused his life to crumble to pieces.

"Jimmie Rivers. I remember. He was found with two bullets in his head behind a business building on Joseph E. Boonc. This guy is pure fucking hell. It's a blessing, but I didn't know he had a daughter."

"My point exactly. There's an entire list of people that you wouldn't know because the lady who's on this transcript as his mother isn't his biological one. He has an entire family with criminal minds and rap sheets long as a fat bitch's ass crack."

"Listen, leave it alone, Berkley. All we have to do is find the girl. The rest of the information has nothing to do with the case at hand," the Captain addressed him, leaning forward.

"Are you fucking kidding me, sir? I think we have a serious situation on our hands. This isn't the average family. I -"

"Will leave it alone. Now you're a great detective and I'm quite sure that there is more to this puzzle that we haven't come across yet. Certain doors aren't meant to be opened. Focus on the girl and take a trip over to the grandmother's high rise. That might help a little."

Closing the folder, Detective Berkley shook his head as he rose to his feet.

"The only way we're gonna find this girl is if we know who we are dealing with. That's not gonna happen if we aren't looking in the right places. Whoever is behind this is someone who's close to her, someone who can reach her at any time. I'm asking you to let me look a little deeper into this."

"And I told you to leave the family research bullshit alone. I don't need any slip-ups falling on this department right now. The feds are ready to pull in and take our jobs at any second and I can't let that happen. Stick to what I told you and find this girl. The rest is history!"

Turning around, Detective Berkley blew out the steam of anger that he held within.

"Berkley?"

"Yes sir?" he asked, stopping in his tracks with the door held open.

"Are we clear on those orders?"

"Yes sir!" was the dry answer he received.

Captain Myers knew his officer well. He watched him as he walked out and headed for the exit. His brain was extra quick and caught on to a lot of things too quickly, things that would turn a happy place into a deathbed of hell. Jimmie Rivers was a person that was better off left dead and never spoken of again.

***

Magic City
11:28 p.m.

The cars and people moved about minute after minute, hour after hour. The lights to the Gentlemen's Club welcomed in some of the friendliest ballers ever. Paper wasn't an issue inside the high class strip joint.

Beno sat across the street parked with his engine silently purring. His lights were off, and he barely leaned back in the seat to keep an eye on the entrance of the club. His skin had been crawling for the answers he wanted to know so badly. Trying to stay focused was becoming impossible. His brain couldn't function without her voice, her touch. The gram of cocaine he had just recently snorted had his paranoia above the limit. The last cop car he spotted was five minutes ago. The crowd began to grow slightly when he spotted his chance.

***

Keith smoothly walked out of the club with the private dancer right on his heels. Moving down the steps, he pulled out the keys to his grey Maserati, deactivating the alarm.

Climbing into the car, he wasted no time grabbing the back of her head and placing his tongue in her mouth. Unbuckling his pants, she instantly got to work at what she did best.

The warmness of her mouth caused him to lean back in satisfaction as she deep throated him. Keith slightly jumped when there was a tap on the window.

"What the fuck?" He panicked, freezing and staring down the barrel of Beno's Glock.

"Roll the window down," Beno calmly said, gripping the pistol lightly.

Keith's chest heaved up and down as he looked over at the woman's terrified face. He pressed the button and the window came down slowly. Beno placed the gun to his cheek.

"Now hold up, brother. If this is a robbery, you can have this shit. Just don't hurt me!"

From the slight crowd that moved in the lot, it looked as if they were having a friendly conversation.

"Where is Reeses?"

"How the fuck am I supposed to know, man? She quit about a week ago. I haven't seen her since."

"That's not the answer I'm looking for."

The first bullet ripped through Keith's jaw, sending blood flying into the woman's face. Her screams caused Beno to release his entire seventeen shots into the car.

The pacing people began to scatter and run towards their cars while Beno calmly walked back across the street to his car.

Getting into the driver's seat, he pulled off in deep thought. The two people who just lost their lives were only a taste of what was racing through his head. He could smell his death approaching but the feelings just didn't matter anymore. Either she was coming back unharmed or he was going out in a casket six feet under.

Chapter 15
8:30 a.m.

The sound of the dog barking caused Reeses to jump out of the deep sleep she was in. Her eyes shifted quickly, looking at the sets of legs coming down the basement steps. The fear inside her stomach locked up as Slick and Quay moved towards her.

Slick jumped into action, backhanding her across the face.

"You stupid little dumb bitch! Where is the fucking money? I've been everywhere and I'm starting to get real fucking impatient," he raged, grasping her face in a tight clench.

Things had gone too far for him. His mind knew that Reeses was playing tricks. His subconscious said to blow her brains on the wall behind her, but he could still taste the millions right at the tip of his fingers.

Reeses knew at that point she might die downstairs inside the filthy basement. She knew his game and it damn sure wasn't gonna play her way if he didn't get what he wanted. No matter what he planned to do, her mind was already made up. She wasn't coming off nothing so that he could win. All the pain and hurt, the suffering he took their family through, was the fuel to her heart.

"Even if I did have anything, I would rather die before I see you with it, motherfucker. You're not gonna get away with this," she spoke with rage glistening in her eyes.

Laughing loudly, Slick slowly massaged his face, looking over at Quay.

"Bring me the chair over here."

Grabbing the seat, he pulled it over towards the center of the floor. Slick placed his hands on Quay's shoulder, making him sit down.

"Now today I'm gonna show you the way we have to handle things for shit to get done. Bitches are very hard headed, and all this does is slow up the process of us receiving our equal share of money. Doesn't that make you mad?" Slick asked, pulling his belt from his pants.

"Hell yeah, that shit makes me mad. I'm tired of wasting time. I need that fucking paper!"

Wrapping the belt around his hand, Slick adjusted just enough length for the buckle to hang freely. Moving swiftly, he stood over Reeses with a demonic smile. Raising his hand, he struck her with the belt across her chest.

She inhaled deeply, feeling the cold buckle connect with her body. The tears gathered in her eyes and tightened her mouth to contain the scream she wanted to release.

"Damn, that shit felt good! You know what? I wanna know what Quay feels about this. Go ahead, Quay, tell Reeses how you feel about your paper. How many days have you been waiting for this shit? How bad you need that money?" he asked. handing him the belt.

"I need my shit really bad. I ain't in this shit for nothing."

"Well, tell that to her." Slick gestured towards Reeses.

Grabbing the belt, Quay wrapped it around his hand. He wasted no time striking her on the side of the head.

Reeses began to scream as Quay hit her repeatedly in her body.

"Aghhhhh!"

"Where the fuck is the paper?" Quay shouted. swinging his hand forcefully.

Trying her best to hide her face, Reeses twirled on her side, feeling the buckle claw at her skin. Before he could land another hit, Slick grabbed his wrist stopping him in action.

"Don't get carried away, my nigga. We still haven't got what the fuck we needed."

Reeses's body felt as if someone had poured gas completely over her and lit the match. No matter how bad she prayed inside of her head, she felt the torture would never end.

"I promise that I would make your life a living nightmare. I was told there was plenty ways to skin a cat and if that cat don't sing, you skin they ass again until they do. Quay, I need you to leave for a minute," Slick said, never taking his eyes off her.

"I'm upstairs if you need me, big bro."

Making his way up the steps, Quay exited the basement leaving Slick to himself.

The silence that loomed in the air was thick. Reeses could hear her heart beat a thousand miles per hour.

"You sure you don't wanna go ahead and tell me what I need to know?" Slick suggested, burning the zip wire from around her feet loose with a small lighter.

Reeses instantly began to move her legs after feeling the tight plastic release from her ankles.

"I told you, I don't have nothing," Reeses spat with a cold face.

Unzipping his pants, he pulled out his private, stoking it in her face. Her body tensed up as he grabbed ahold of her legs.

"Get the fuck off me!" she cried, trying to break free from his grasp.

Slick replied with a hard right fist to her jaw. The dizziness overpowered her vision, causing her to blank out.

***

Madison Village Apartments
9:32 a.m.

"Bruh, you've been sitting here an entire night and still haven't come up with nothing. Our sister is still out there, and you just stopped me while I was in my motion yesterday. In order to get answers, you gotta make motherfuckers talk, Justin," Phil said, sitting in a chair on the opposite side of the room.

Justin remained quiet, staring out of the window beside him.

"All these pussy-ass niggas is out here cheating death. Your friend, a.k.a. high school buddy, tried to fuck Reeses. Now I'm not a genius, but we can both agree that our sister is a little developed for her age. It's a big difference when she was only fifteen, smart guy. You've heard all you need to know."

"Yeah, you right. I've heard a lot, Phil. What about your right-hand man Malik? You've heard the same shit about him, I know, and I haven't seen you mention his name one time," Justin said calmly.

"You have to be the dumbest nigga in the world if you think I exclude any one of these pussy fiending-ass niggas out of this situation. I've been in my cell the past week thinking of who I would murder on the strength and you think I'm giving passes to a motherfucker?"

"I don't know what you've been thinking. All I know is our sister needs us and if we're gonna find her, we have to come a little more silent then we have come. Now do you really want to keep taking chances and just cause destruction, or do you wanna move the way Pops coached us?"

Standing up, Phil placed his gun under his shirt and laughed.

"Unfortunately, my father has been dead for ten years. It's no coaching when it comes to someone trying to harm us. It's only one way. Now are you gonna help me find our sister or not?" he asked with an aggravated expression.

Trying to keep his faith in Allah's ways was one issue, but the negative jinn his brother carried was starting to spill off into him. He didn't want the old Jack he contained in his system to re-surface.

Grabbing his gun off the coffee table, he retrieved his extra clip and looked at his brother.

"I hope you're ready to deal with the reaction that's gonna come behind this."

Opening the front door, Phil smiled wickedly.

"Now that sounds like my brother talking."

They made their way out. The city was about to feel Jimmie reincarnated. Time was too valuable to let pass. If blood was what it took to get Reeses back, then Jack and Poker would ensure everyone involved would surely pay with their life.

***

After placing on his Ferragamo belt, Malik stared into the bedroom mirror and rubbed his hands through his thick waves. Today was his time to shine and prove that he was the true hustler and he had what it took to be in the game.

"Malik, you need to come eat this shit before it gets cold," he heard his baby mama yell from the dining room.

Putting wheat colored Timberland boots on his feet, he made his way towards the front.

"It's nice of you to join us for a change," Monica teased, knowing he would be gone soon.

Kissing his son on the forehead, he pecked her lips softly and took the seat beside her.

"I see you got good jokes early in the morning."

"Nah, it's beyond a joke. How many more times do you have to do this?"

"I told you one time already, ma, I'm doing this to make sure we get straight. It's not gonna be for long," he replied nonchalantly, fixing a plate.

"It doesn't take long at all to get hurt or end up in a prison cell either."

He shook his head. He knew the conversation was about to head in a different direction.

***

Phil pulled down into the Carriage Home Apartments and slowed the car down.

"He's upstairs in apartment three."

"How do we even know if he's home or not?" Justin asked, looking around at the quiet residence.

"We take our ass up there and see!"

Opening the car door, Phil stepped out and Justin followed. They maneuvered their way to the top floor.

"So what, you just gon' knock on the door, ask the nigga where our sister is at, and kill him on the front porch?"

"Not if he don't make me," Phil spat, twisting the doorknob.

The door opened quietly, surprising both of them. Looking at each other, they pulled their guns and slowly crept inside.

***

"Listen, I told you one time before that if you ain't gonna help me get this paper, then I will get out here and do it myself. I'm tired of having to spit this same ole shit," Malik shouted.

Monica was about to reply to his comment, but froze in fear from the two men who turned into their dining room.

Malik stared into the eyes of two killers he could never forget. His heartbeat began to slow down and the guns they held caused his stomach to grumble loudly.

"Poker, Jack? How in the fuck did y'all get into my house?"

Monica grabbed her three-year-old son and pulled him close, watching Justin take a seat at the table.

"That doesn't matter anymore. We're here. We need to know the last time you've seen our little sister. Malik. Just because we've been gone doesn't mean we don't have our ear to the streets. Seems like the whole crew was interested in fucking minors," Justin said dryly.

"I never touched you niggas' sister, not one time in my fucking life. That's on my son, bro."

"Bae, what the fuck is going on? What are these men doing in our house and what do you have to do with this woman?" Monica mumbled with a terrified expression.

"Bro, I don't know what y'all have heard, but it's a lie. The last person I saw your sister with was the li'l nigga who stay across the street from her. He's always with her 24/7. She threw a party at her spot and that's how I met this dude. She danced with me once and I told her I didn't feel comfortable, so she stopped. I know y'all have been gone for a long time, but I'm still the same Malik," he pleaded. trying to dodge his way out of be misunderstood situation.

"What's his name?" Phil asked. leaning gently on the wall.

"I don't know."

Justin stared deep in his eyes and could tell that he was telling the truth. From the look of the frightened child and woman, they were just as clueless. Something wasn't adding up and too many mixed signals were being thrown into the game.

"You wouldn't mind taking a ride with us to point out exactly who we are dealing with? Would you?"

Phil didn't hesitate to aim at Malik's head with his 40-caliber, ordering him outside. His wife and child began to panic as Justin stood directly in front of them.

"Please, all you have to do is relax. We're not gonna hurt him as long as he cooperates. I need you to stay away from the phones and remain in the house. If you listen, your husband will be back within an hour unharmed. Do you understand?"

Holding her child tightly, Monica nodded.

"I promise," Justin assured her before walking out.

Chapter 16

Beno slowed his Challenger down as he parked in front of his two-bedroom home. The heavy bags under his eyes were confirmation that he hadn't slept in days.

Stepping out of his whip, gun in hand, he paused, looking at the three men heading towards him.

"Say, li'l bro? Do you mind if we holla at you for a minute?" Justin asked humbly, noticing the gun that was dangling in his palm.

"Yeah, I mind a lot. Do you mind telling me why the fuck you niggas are posted in front of my door?" Beno replied with a screwed face.

Ignoring his attitude, Justin began to speak his peace.

"This is Phil and I'm Justin. I know it may seem a little strange with us sitting in front of your door, but we was led here by a reliable source and we thought you might could help us. We're looking for our sister Reeses."

"Sister? I've heard about Reeses's brothers and they're in prison, so you can try that shit with somebody else. You clown-ass niggas need to get the fuck away from here."

Phil eased his gun out, returning the same aggression back towards him.

"Listen, my nigga. If we wanted to kill yo' busta ass, we could've done it when you first pulled up. We're looking for our baby sister. Short, brown skin, grey eyes with long black hair. We're just now getting out of prison so it's impossible for you to know who the fuck we are. If you did know, you probably would cut the tough guy role and tell us exactly what you know so we could be on our way."

Malik sat quietly behind them with his head down, staying far away from the conversation as he could. He knew if things went wrong, there was a possibility that he wouldn't make it home to his wife and child.

Walking into Phil's face, Beno stood eye to eye with him before he spoke.

"I've been around Reeses since she was in middle school. I love her with all my heart. I've been maneuvering around this city killing anything that moves to get her back home. Maybe your niggas ain't got ya ears to the street as good as you did before you left, because if you did, you would know that I'm gonna tear this bitch down until I find her. So if you niggas ain't on the same shit that I'm on, stay the fuck out of my way and I'll find her on my own."

Justin stepped into the conversation before Phil could open his mouth. His temper was beyond normal and any help at this point to find Reeses was the only thing flooding through his brain.

"Look, we mean no harm. I can see that you care for our sister just as we do. Do you have any idea on who could have done this?"

"No. Reeses doesn't bother with too many people. I came home one day, and I found her house totally trashed. The people who I had in mind are already dead."

"Hold up! How we don't know this lame-ass nigga ain't got nothing to do with this shit?" Phil said, breaking his silence and pointing at Beno.

"Fuck you, nigga! You don't know shit about me. Reeses is all I care about. Neither one of you niggas mean shit. Now if you niggas could please get the fuck away from in front of my door, I can continue my mission," Beno said with a stale face.

"Wait a minute. I think there's a lot more to this story than all of us truly know. Just take my number. If you hear anything, contact me. We're not gonna be able to find anything out going at each other. Someone has to know something."

Beno looked down at the paper as if it was poison. Taking it out of his hand, he nodded his head and walked towards the house.

"If you ask me, that nigga knows something. You should've let me shoot his ass just to see if he would come up with a different story then," Phil mumbled arrogantly.

"Trust me, whatever him and Reeses has going on is past friends. I can feel the pain coming off his voice when he spoke about her. He's lost, just like we are," Justin disagreed.

"You know just like I know who has the juice around this motherfucker. We need to push up and see if he knows because we aren't getting anywhere."

Justin looked over at Malik and could smell the nervousness crawling on his skin.

"You no longer have anything else to do with this. Go back home to your family, bro."

Malik wasted no time taking off jogging down the street. His heart raced quickly as he ducked his head, in fear of being shot.

Phil pulled his pistol quickly, aiming at Malik's back. Before his finger could pull the trigger, Justin stopped him in motion.

"Nigga, what the fuck are you doing? That fuckboy needs to die. He can rat on us!" Phil raged, watching at Malik bend the corner.

"He's not gonna tell, Phil. He's not the person we are after. We need to save this energy for whoever actually has Reeses."

"Aye, listen, nigga! When I pull my fucking strap, don't ever stop me from busting my gun. You got your way and I got mines."

Snatching his gun away, he moved towards the car and climbed inside the passenger seat.

No matter how Phil felt at that moment, Justin knew that they were getting close. So many people knew of the reputation of the Rivers that they wouldn't even dare to make the move that was at hand. Shaun's face popped in his head as he got inside the driver seat and pulled off.

***

Paradise East Apartments

Blue stood posted on the sidewalk of the driveway. Digging in his blue Balmain fitted jeans, he pulled out his lighter, sparking the end of the Cali kush. The Rolac Blood gang members posted up on the side of the porch, shooting dice for the honchos that laid on the ground. Paradise East was the spot to head to if you really wanted to make some extra paper. If you weren't homie of S.M.M., you probably would have to know someone just to step inside.

"Yooo, Blue?" the young hustler yelled out, stepping onto the porch.

"If it isn't the little demon himself. Wassup with it, li'l bro?"

"The same shit every day. Dodge all the fake-ass negativity. Fuck me some thoties and get some paper. Speaking of wassup, what the hell been going on with ya cousin?" he asked with a curious expression.

"Who?"

"Nigga, Beno. This nigga been riding around killing shit for like three days now."

Blue stared at the young kid strangely before he burst out into deep laughter.

"Bruh, you might got the wrong Beno. My cousin is not a fucking killer. He just sells a little work and is starting to get a little paper. That's it."

"Nigga, I got the right person. Beno that drives the blue Challenger now. Your cousin who we went to school with. That nigga been out here on the bullshit. Something about his girl getting kidnapped made him snap and he been tripping since then."

After hitting his blunt again, the words started to set into Blue's head. "What did you just say?"

"Nigga, you ain't listen? I said yo' cousin killing - "

"Not that. About the kidnapping of the girl."

"I told you, his girl got taken or some shit like that. He must have been fucking with this chick kind of strong 'cause lately he been on some real grim reaper shit."

"Fuck that. What does the bitch look like?" Blue asked desperately.

"Goddamn my nigga, chill. It's a little cute-ass brown chick. She thick, about five feet tall with grey eyes. I think her name Buttercup or some shit like that."

Walking off the porch, Blue felt the bad energy from those words run through his body. The sight of the tied up woman in the basement was a day he never forgot. The memory of her eye color wasn't positive to him, but the description was too ambiguous.

Strolling to his car, he got in and placed a call to Quay.

"Yo, what the fuck you want, busta?"

"Where the fuck you at, man?" Blue asked, starting his engine.

"The same place I been all week. I'm over here with a couple of homies. Slide up through here."

"I'm on the way."

Hanging up his cell, he made his way towards the spot. If his mind wasn't playing tricks on him, he knew that things were about to get extremely out of hand.

***

Parking in front of the trap headquarters, Blue stepped out of the Ford Taurus, straightening his Philly snapback. Even though the sun was still up, the November wind cut through his jacket, matching the chills of nervousness flowing from his aura.

He knocked on the front door and it was instantly opened, allowing him access inside. The young goon who answered held an AK-47 assault rifle in his left hand. The look on his face spelled fuckery and the way his hand gripped the trigger spoke for his gangsta.

"Where is Quay?" Blue asked, standing in the living room looking at the two hittas in front of him.

Lady, the red pitbull, began to bark viciously, sensing a new presence in the crib.

"Bro, downstairs in the basement. He is waiting on you," one of the hustlers replied, taking a seat on the couch.

Maneuvering his way inside the kitchen, Blue opened the side door and headed downstairs.

"Goddamn, nigga. It took you long enough," Quay teased, sipping his cup of Activist.

Greez sat down directly beside him at the table, bagging up raw cocaine. Word on the street was that Greez had murdered six people inside of an apartment over a bad conversation. He was a guy that was never to be trusted. He never spoke around people he didn't like and if he was with Quay, there was trouble in the atmosphere.

"I was right around the corner. Who are the new cats running the door upstairs?"

"Some li'l shooters I linked up with from the temp. Slick been asking me to put this team together and soon it's not gon' be nothing that can stop this shit," Quay said.

Looking to his right, Blue locked eyes with Reeses and felt the certainty in his heart. Her brown skin glowed even though her lips craved water and her grey eyes were begging silently for help. Her description was a match.

"So, wassup with this fine li'l-ass bitch that's been in the corner for the past couple of days? Is she fucking or what?" Blue asked, walking towards her.

"When Slick tells me to make a move, that's when we'll know, and she ain't trying to fuck nothing willingly." Quay laughed, counting the sacks of dope.

Bending down in front of her, Blue's eyes demanded her to pay attention. Looking down, she spotted the small switchblade dangling in his hand. Her body stiffened in fear, but his vibe just didn't give off the bad energy she knew was coming to her. Quickly placing the knife in her lap, she pulled her legs in close to her hands.

"I'm gonna help you," he mumbled lightly.

Her eyes began to slightly tear up as she nodded her head.

"What the fuck are you doing? Praying over the bitch?" Quay asked, standing behind him.

Slightly jumping, he stood to his feet and adjusted his hat.

"Hell nah, nigga. I'm just playing with the li'l hoe that's all. Why the hell you so close up on me?"

Before he could step to the side, Quay pulled his gun, placing it to Blue's chest.

"You sure you a'ight, my nigga? You been acting real strange lately. Is there something I need to know?"

Blue's body locked, feeling the hard steel pressed against his heart. "Quay! I don't know what the fuck you been smoking, but you fucking trippin. Take this gun away from my chest before you accidently shoot me."

Blue's legs started to quiver upon witnessing Greez holding onto his Glock with a slight grin.

Lowering his gun, Quay flashed a cheesy fake smile. "Nigga, shut yo' scary ass up. You just almost shitted on yo'self. Greez, let's hit the living room and smoke with these clowns. It's already pass 4:30 and I don't need to be too fucked up when all this traffic start pouring in."

"Look, man, I'ma catch y'all niggas later. I'm about to get on the road and finish handling my business for today," Blue lied.

"Damn, bruh, you just now sliding through. Yo' duck ass done let one of these bitches trick you," Quay joked as the three men headed up the basement steps.

Blue continued to remain silent until he left out the front door. His hands slightly shook while he treaded to his car and got in. His paranoia radar was skyrocket high and there was only one decision to make. How was he going to tell Beno?

Chapter 17

Walking into the small two bedroom apartment, Slick stepped over the dirty junkies that lay about freely. The smell of smoked crack was looming thick in the air.

"Where she at?" Slick asked the basehead who sat at the raggedy dining room table.

"She in the back. Are we still straight on the money I owe you, Slick? I need me a front until my check come on the first."

Ignoring her thirst for the drug, he made his way to the bedroom and walked inside.

Tasha sat in the filthy bed, picking at the dry skin that covered her arm. Her hair was shedding as if she had been diagnosed with cancer. Her once perfect body had vanished drastically thanks to her new best friend named heroin.

"Bitch, stop playing with me. I know you see me standing right here, Tasha. Tell me what I need to know so I can go on about my business."

"Please don't hurt me anymore, Slick. I'm so tired of running. I told you everything I know the last time you saw me," she replied, looking at him with an exhausted face.

"You didn't tell me enough. I've been running through this entire city and I still haven't found a trace of this money. There's obviously something you're forgetting to mention, Tasha. Now do we have to do this the easy way or the hard way?" Slick asked, exposing the handle of his gun.

"You told me that you wouldn't hurt her, Slick. She's like a daughter to me, for Christ sake!" Tasha whispered with pain in her voice.

"I wouldn't give a fuck if she was your biological seed. You're the only thing that's holding me back from this payday and if you think I came this far to lose, I will kill her with no hesitation."

"Your soul is cold for a reason. It will be the same reason God will have a cold heart and watch you burn in hell for eternity. What's the point of telling you anything if you're still gonna hurt that girl, Slick?"

"She won't get hurt if you cooperate like you supposed to," he replied, tossing an ounce of heroin on the bed.

The monkey that climbed her back began to kick forcefully. Her palms began to sweat while she rubbed her arm back and forth.

"It's only one person Reeses will trust with that money. If you find that boy she hangs under, you gon' find everything."

"What the fuck are you talking about? What boy?"

"All you have to do is ask Blue. He knows," Tasha said truthfully, opening the bag of drugs.

Walking out of the room, Slick instantly jumped on his cell to make a call.

"Yo, what's good, big bruh?" Quay answered.

"Where's Blue? Is he around you?" Slick asked, making his way quickly to the car.

"Nah, he just left. Said he had to handle some business or some shit and he'll be back later. Why?"

"If he comes back, hold him there and call me. If he tries to buck, shoot him. Just don't kill him."

"Done," Quay replied, hanging up.

The deeds were done and now it was time to collect the benefits. Whoever decided to place their life in jeopardy for the money was on borrowed time - family or friend.

***

"Baby, please! Think about our son. If we lose you, who else is gonna help our family get by, huh?" Monica pleaded.

"Man, fuck that. These niggas came in my house and placed a gun to my head in front of my kid. Both of them bitch-ass niggas gotta die!" Malik yelled, moving back and forth.

His mind couldn't take the fact that his manhood was just tested in front of his own family. Poker and Jack were two people who he considered true friends. He knew that gangsta shit ran through their blood, but there was no way in hell he was gonna let them ruin the reputation he took years to build.

"Your pride is in the way with this issue. You should be glad you're still alive. You said these dudes just got out of prison. If they are doing this, what makes you think they care about going back?"

"Just get out and let me think, Monica. Can you just leave me the fuck alone for five minutes?"

Folding her arms, she stormed out of the room, slamming the door behind her.

Malik sat at the end of his bed and pondered. He knew that his hands were tied. Pressing the green button on his phone, he listened to it ring twice before it was picked up.

"Smyrna Police Department. This is Officer Judy West. What is the crime you are calling to report?" the woman spoke fluently.

His stomach began to crumble before he spoke the words.

"I'm calling to report evidence about a murder. I have reason to believe that they may harm someone else again."

"Sir, hold on while I transfer your call to our shift leader."

He heard the line click and ring, and his call was immediately accepted.

"This is Detective Berkley. What is the name of the victim you are trying to report sir?"

"Margaret Myers."

Hearing the name, Berkley sat straight up in his seat.

"Sir, do you think you can possibly come to the precinct and speak to me directly?"

"I'll be there in twenty minutes," Malik replied, hanging up while he walked out of his room.

"Malik, what are you about to do?" Monica asked, standing up from the living room couch.

"I'm about to make sure these niggas will regret ever fucking with us," he answered before leaving.

***

Leaning over the rail of the apartment balcony, Justin stared at the illuminating lights that danced across all the buildings. Faith was beginning to fade, but giving up was something that wasn't in his vision.

Pulling on his Newport Light, thoughts of Reeses flashed through his brain back to back. He wondered hard on who would actually have enough guts to try and harm a member of the Rivers family. Regardless of Jimmie being gone, their reputation stood strong and held major weight from Atlanta to Tennessee. Their laws were laid years before they went to prison, but losing their parents in the same year started the disaster to their legacy. In the back of Justin's head, he could feel Reeses was still alive. The pieces that they so badly needed were still missing.

Justin looked behind him as Phil stepped through the glass door.

"Wassup with it, Farrakhan? You wanna get out of here in these streets tonight or what?" Phil asked, lighting the green leaf he had between his lips.

"I'm trying to think before we make a move like this. I think we're really looking over the pointers of our situation."

"And we've been through the so-called pointers a hundred times, bro. The fact of the matter is we have to be prepared for the possibility that our little sister may be dead. Open mouths leave a casket or burial and people just aren't into dying these days. We will know when we find our guy when he starts to sing like a yellow canary."

"That's understood. Answer me a question. Who are considered the best thieves and killers?" Justin asked with his mind on something else.

"The unseen."

"Exactly! It's only my conscience eating at me to tell us the way. Shaun knows. He's been missing in action ever since we stepped out of those prison walls. He knew we were coming home this month. I even talked to him a while back and told him to keep an eye out on Reeses."

"Well why in the fuck are we still sitting here? Let's go and push up on this nigga to see what the fuck he knows."

"That's the problem. We can't just do that, Poker. Shaun is extremely paranoid and if he feels we came to hurt him, he's gonna react the wrong way."

"If he's missing in action, he obviously already knows, Justin. You act like you scared of this nigga or something."

"I've never been scared of any man in my life. I'm just moving smart. Certain chances we make will be with us forever and I'm not about to make the wrong one for anybody."

***

Blue sat on the front of his porch, inhaling the weed smoke from the Dutch master deeply. His heart was scared to hear the truth, but there wasn't any other way. Dialing Beno's number, he sat back until he got an answer.

"Hello?"

"Listen, cuz, I know you have a lot of shit going on and I been hearing a lot of crazy shit running through the streets. Who is this girl that's supposed to be missing? I need you to tell me what's going on," Blue asked with concern in his voice.

Nothing but silence could be heard through the line until Beno took a deep breath.

"It's a lot going on right now, Blue, and I don't need people all in my business. For the past few days, I've been riding around looking for my girl. I'm fucking worried about her, bro. Word is she got snatched up and been missing ever since."

"Why haven't you told me about this earlier? What does this girl look like, Beno?"

"She's brown-skinned with grey eyes. Her name is Reeses."

Hearing the confirmation from the horse's mouth, Blue's heart began to beat furiously.

"I gots to find her, Blue. I'm gonna tear this city down until I do," Beno stated.

"Listen, I think I can help you. I'm gonna call you right back."

"What? What do you mean help me? Have you heard something?" Beno asked, feeling his vibe.

"I might be able to help. Just give me a minute."

"Tell me what the fuck is going on, Blue."

Hanging up in his face, Blue rubbed his hands through his hair. Shit was serious and getting killed by his own cousin wasn't in the plan. He knew that Quay would rather die before he handed over his so-called come up. Blue knew the only way out of the situation was to stay far away from it.

Chapter 18

Reeses opened her eyes slightly after hearing the footsteps head back upstairs. Her adrenaline was at a high volume. Her mind and body were so tired, but her brain wouldn't let her rest. The knife she clutched in her hand was her only hope and today she was praying she got her chance to escape from the trap that contained her.

Moving into action, she used the knife to scrape across the thick zip ties. Her fingers only pushed so far from the restraints choking down on her wrist. Beads of sweat began to form across her forehead while the knife slightly bit through the synthetic thermoplastic. She began to twist her wrist, working the blade with her hands to get free. She listened carefully to the footsteps that moved above her head. Her heart skipped a beat when the tie popped, freeing her hands. She quickly moved down towards her feet, cutting through the thick material. Tears slowly rolled down her face after the material broke loose.

Getting to her feet slowly, she looked across the room at her phone sitting on the glass table and rushed towards it. Her hands trembled. Quickly opening the phone up to Beno's missed calls, she dialed his number. Her chest heaved up and down as she prayed for an answer.

"Hello? Hello?" Beno asked in a breathless tone.

"Beno! Baby, help me!" Reeses whispered, letting the pain out in silent tears.

"Reeses, baby! Where are you? Tell me where you are?" he asked, yelling with hurt in his tone.

"I don't know. My uncle kidnapped me. I'm in a basement of someone's house." She panicked, listening closely to the front door of the home open and close.

***

"Is there any other place you know this nigga would be?" Slick asked Quay as they stood inside the living room.

"The only place I can say off the top of my head is his mama's. I knew that bitch-ass fuck nigga's been acting weird lately. He's obviously the reason we haven't got ahold of this paper yet," Quay responded, looking at the three other men who stood beside them.

"Fuck all that! Once I get my hands on his pussy ass, he gon' tell me everything we need to know, or he gon' take a dirt nap right beside that bitch. Greez, come ride with me. Quay, you stay here with these two and watch that bitch. Keep this shit running. After we get this money today, we slumping these folks and moving to a different location."

"I got you, my nigga," Quay replied, sipping the codeine in his Styrofoam.

After Slick left the spot, Quay smiled to himself, knowing that the sweet lick was approaching. All he had to do was get his hands on the money, he thought as he strolled towards the basement.

***

"Baby, do you see any windows or anything you can protect yourself with? Tell me, what do you see?"

She looked around the room. Her thoughts ran a full mile as she tried to think over the loud dog that was barking above her.

"It's nothing around me, Beno. I can't think with the dog barking."

"What did you say?" he asked, feeling his heart drop.

As the feet above her moved across the floor, she instantly grew more nervous.

"Beno, he's coming. Please help me," Reeses whispered before hanging up.

Setting the phone back on the table, she quickly moved back to the corner as the basement door came open.

Walking down the steps, Quay smiled with a wicked expression, tasting the drugs in his cup.

"Today's that day, li'l mama. We have suffered long enough waiting on you to do the right thing. It's gonna feel good to kill you and watch the life drain outta yo' ass," Quay spat, sitting in the chair at the glass table. Removing his gun, he clutched it in his hand, staring at her seductively. "I hate that I couldn't get a chance to feel how warm that little coochie of yours is. You should have just come off that shit the first time and you probably could be lying in my bed somewhere."

Reeses stared at him with cold eyes. Her knees were pulled into her chest and she held the pocket blade tightly in her palm without saying a word. Her heart could feel the cold fate that awaited her. If she didn't make it out of this place today, she knew there was a chance she would never be seen again.

***

Beno moved around the house, on edge. His chest felt as if it would explode when he heard her sweet voice come through his line. He knew that she was alive, and she needed him. Clutching his pistol tightly, he snorted a line of cocaine to boost his adrenaline rush. As he sat down on the couch, the words that replayed inside his head made his skin turn cold.

"I can't think with the dog barking."

The conclusion smashed into him, causing him to dial Blue's number quickly. His fingers were clutched so tightly that his nails began to dig inside his palm.

"Hello?" Blue answered in a low voice.

"I'm gonna ask you one time and one time only. Is my girl inside your spot?" Beno asked, praying that he heard the right answer.

"Beno, listen to me. I don't have anything to do with this. I - "

"Answer my fucking question, Blue! Is Reeses over there? Is my girl inside of that house?"

"Beno, I'm sorry, cuz. I didn't mean for it to come out this way. I was trying to help."

"When I catch you, I'm going to kill you," he replied, grabbing his gun and heading out the door.

***

Blue sat inside his mother's blue Toyota, still holding the phone as if Beno's voice was coming back. He rubbed his eyes. He knew that his cousin was in love with this girl from the way he spoke. He cursed himself for not letting her loose the moment when he had a chance.

A loud knock on the car window startled him, causing his eyes to look directly at the devil himself. Slick motioned for him to unlock the door, waving his pistol lightly without saying a word. Blue's first intention was to crank the car and smash off. His mind told him to do it, but his hands wouldn't jump into action.

Looking to his left, he spotted Greez treading up the small flight of stairs straight to his front door. After viewing his mom open the door only to be pushed back inside, he unlocked the car door.

Slick climbed into the passenger seat and closed the distance between him and Blue immediately. His face was close enough to see the evil and murder mentality pour drastically out of his pupils.

"Wassup, Blue? Why haven't I been seeing you, my nigga? We been over here at the spot trying to make this money and you've been missing in action."

"Hell nah! It's nothing like that, big bro. I've just got a lot of extra bullshit going on. Why did Greez just go in my house?" he asked with a look of concern on his face.

"He just needed to use the restroom. Trust me, that's not the problem that we are focused on at this moment."

"What problem?" Blue asked, already realizing the foul play that was about to go down.

Pulling out his black silencer, Slick began to twist it on the front of the handgun slowly.

"I'm gonna ask you a few questions, Blue. It's all up to you if your mother walks back out of that house again."

Blue could feel his heart thumping through his chest rapidly. His eyes bulged, watching Slick as he placed the deadly weapon on his lap.

"Tell me, who's the girl's boyfriend? Or tell me where my money is. Now before you think about giving me a bullshitting pussy-ass excuse, consider your mother's life, Blue."

The words stumbled terribly out of his lips as he tried to gather his lie. His intention was to save his mother's life, but betraying Beno came with the same price.

Sensing that he was playing, Slick placed the gun to his head and slowly pulled back on the hammer.

"First I'm gonna have Greez chop up your mama while you watch. Next, I'm gonna beat you to a pulp, stick a broom handle up ya ass, and shoot you in the back of the head. Last chance," Slick taunted, flickering his finger on the trigger lightly.

"Okay!" Blue fidgeted, closing his eyes tightly.

***

Detective Berkley made his way inside of the office, quickly moving towards the interrogation room. He held the confidential file inside of his hand as he scanned the room to make sure Captain Myers was far out of sight.

Strolling through the door, he closed it behind him and took his seat across from Malik, who waited patiently.

"Mr. Robertson, I've taken drastic measures to stop my day and listen to the information that you say is important for the police department of Smyrna to know. I'm going to record this session and this information will only be kept between me and you. Your safety matters."

Pressing record on the tape player, he placed it towards the middle section of the table. "Can you please state your name for me, sir?"

"Malik Robertson."

"Okay, Mr. Robertson, tell me exactly what you are trying to report."

"I want to report a murder, and I have reason to believe that these people will strike again."

"And do you know the name of this victim?"

"Margaret Myers."

Hearing the name slide through his head and ears caused his skin to crawl. The room seemed to grow quiet while Berkley looked him directly in the eyes. "Sir, when did this murder take place?"

"October 18, 2007."

"Sir, you do know that Margaret Myers is an unsolved murder. We haven't been able to crack it in ten years."

Malik nodded his head, assuring Berkley that he understood.

Getting out of his seat, Berkley locked the office door and closed the blinds. "I need you to understand exactly what you're doing at this time. This is a very delicate case. Do you know the person who did this?" he asked, leaning on the table.

"Justin and Philip Rivers," Malik stated with a "for sure" expression.

Detective Berkley didn't know if it was meant to be that he was in the office on the right day upon hearing the names involved. He knew there was officially a cold case file that was about to be re-opened.

Stopping the tape recorder, he stared at Malik with a blank face.

"I need you to tell me everything you know from the start."

"They ran by the names Jack and Poker," Malik started off.

Chapter 19

After Quay retrieved his cup from upstairs, he made his way back down to the basement. Sparking his half of the joint, he calmly walked over to Reeses, staring down at her.

"I would ask you do you wanna taste a little of this, but you already been leaning a few days." He laughed, stumbling slightly.

Reeses held eye contact with him, praying that he didn't notice her legs were untied.

"Can you really believe that after this move, I'm gonna be able to earn me a spot as kingpin around this muthafucka? Kicking doors in for flat screens and jewelry is getting boring," Quay said, moving towards the hardwood chair by the table.

Removing his pistol from his waist, he sat down and pointed it towards Reeses's head. Tilting the cup to his lips, he took a quick sip and shook his head slowly.

"The sad part about it, li'l mama, is you ain't the only one who about to suffer in this shit. Slick is gonna feel this shit too. If two people are dead, the last nigga that's alive ain't gotta worry about no one snitching on him but hisself."

"Can you please just let me go? Slick is making you believe that you're gonna receive money that you are never going to see. I will give you thirty thousand dollars if you just release me," Reeses said in a sincere tone.

"Release you? Thirty thousand? I've been sitting in a basement with you for a week. I take the precious time out of my day to help you to the toilet, feed you, and plenty more. I've played with the pussy twice and all I get is thirty bands? It's not enough," Quay shouted in a drunken slur.

Lighting his cigarette, he leaned his head back in satisfaction. The Xanax bars he had popped earlier started to kick in hard, causing him to get slightly drowsy.

"After I get this money, I'm killing everybody," he mumbled to himself, tasting the harsh nicotine again.

He gazed at her from a spaced out zone. He closed his eyes for a short second and then re-opened them. The cancer stick in his hand fell from in between his fingers to the floor.

Reeses stared at him quietly, watching his mouth open partially. His eyes closed again as he fell into a slight snooze.

Reeses' vision began to focus on the handgun that was dangling from his palm.

All she could think about was getting out of the basement alive. Everything around her began to fade as she focused in on Quay. Hearing the small snore that escaped his lips gave her the courage to slowly get to her feet.

Gripping her blade in her hand tightly, she knew it was either her or him.

***

Beno gripped the handle of his M-16 assault rifle. He could feel the rage flowing through his body as he turned, speeding down Gresham Road.

Spotting the green home, he jumped out quickly with the rifle aimed straight out in front of him. His eyes observed the surroundings of the home before he stepped on the front porch, kicking the door in.

The first person he spotted was a young goon on the living room couch. His finger squeezed the trigger, sending eight shots directly through the center of his body.

Walking over to him, Beno placed the gun to his head and sent one more slug through his skull.

The bullet that struck his arm caused him to jump behind the large couch. A young worker popped his gun rapidly, trying to hit whatever he could as he hid behind the corner of the wall.

"You ran into the wrong spot, pussy-ass nigga. You don't know who you fucking with!" he screamed, letting off another round.

Beno bit on his bottom lip, feeling the blood ooze down from his forearm. All his mind could see was an image of Reeses's face needing his help. She was all he had left, and there was nothing that could stop him from holding her in his arms again.

Clutching the gun, he rose to his feet quietly and began to spray the entire wall with a gang of bullets.

"Ahh shit!" the shooter yelled, feeling a burning sensation rip through the top of his back.

Beno made his move, walking swiftly around the corner. The man lay on his back, breathing erratically, trying to reach for his gun.

Stepping on top of the handgun, Beno positioned this assault rifle between the man's eyes. "Where is Reeses?" he asked in a low voice.

"Fuck you, nigga. You and that bitch still gon' get what's coming to y'all. Slick ain't stopping until he gets all that bread."

"You won't be here to see it," Beno spat, releasing a bullet into the middle of his forehead.

Raising the gun back up, he slowly made his way down the hallway.

***

Reeses took her last step, standing directly over Quay. Raising the knife, she jumped upon hearing the gunfire that erupted upstairs.

Quay opened his eyelids, looking up at Reeses, who bore down on him with hate in her eyes, plunging the knife into the top of his collarbone. Quay dropped his gun and reached for her arms. Pressing her weight against him, she stuck him repeatedly, watching his eyes glow in pain.

"Son of a bitch!" she screamed, jumping off him and watching his body fall helplessly.

Snatching his gun off the floor, she moved towards the corner, watching Quay as he tried his best to breathe out slowly. The gunshots upstairs continued to ring out, confusing her as to the next move she was about to make. After watching Quay's body movement cease, she knew any minute somebody could come rushing down the steps to kill her.

After hearing the shots cease, her heart quacked with pure fear. Grabbing her phone, she placed it inside her bra and held the gun with two hands, heading up the first few steps. Hearing nothing but silence still, she roamed to the top and placed her ear to the door.

Grabbing the handle, she turned the knob and cracked the door to see if she could view anything. Her chest pounded heavily as the door flew open.

"Baby?" Beno said, dropping his M-16 on the floor, embracing her.

"Beno?" she replied, feeling that she was dreaming.

"It's okay, ma, I'm here."

The tears couldn't help but pour down her bruised cheeks while she stared into his eyes. "You really came for me," she sobbed, holding him tightly.

"I told you I would never leave you, Reeses. You're all I have left. I gots to get you out of here," he replied, picking up the gun from the floor.

They made their way down the hallway. Reeses closed her eyes to block out the gruesome scene inside the living room. The sun instantly warmed her skin when they stepped out on the porch. Beno held her close until he got to the car, placing her on the passenger side. Moving to the driver's door, he climbed in and sped off, thanking God the worst was finally over.

***

First Baptist Church
1275 Church Street

Shaun stepped out of the church doors just as the rain started to drizzle down out of the sky. His son and daughter came down the steps, moving quickly towards the car.

"I hope you don't think you gonna be out standing on no block tonight either. You said it's our family night, so I don't want to hear shit about making no moves." His girl beamed into his eyes.

"Sugar, I told you my word is bond, but what you have to understand is we gotta survive. I'm gonna take care of you guys no matter what the cost behind it."

Smiling, Sugar leaned in, kissing his lips softly. Her smile turned to a huge frown upon spotting the two identical men leaning across their car. Phil held the hands of the two small children while Justin held his pistol close to his side.

Shaun's face went from happiness to war mode upon spotting his two childhood enemies. Moving Sugar behind him, he placed his hands on the handle of his 9mm Glock handgun.

"Please, Shaun, don't do it. We only wanna talk to you," Justin warned, exposing his Springfield XD3 handgun fully.

"Don't seem like y'all niggas wanna talk with my kids standing next to y'all. Don't make me do this shit, Jack," he replied with a stare as cold as ice.

Phil pulled his pistol around the young boy's chest. "Move ya fucking hand before I blow his shit all the way to the altar, fuck nigga."

"Shaun! What the fuck is going on? Who are those men holding my children?" Sugar asked, ready to panic upon seeing the guns.

Placing his hands down by his side, Shaun cracked his neck from side to side. He knew that Jack and Poker were true with their words. He knew their gangsta was as official as his own. "I'm listening!" he said with hostility.

"Reeses is missing. We've been looking for her for the past four days and still can't find her. Word in the street is you might be able to tell us something to help us out a little."

"You niggas are fucking stupid. You really think you can come draw guns on my family and expect me to help you with something that you should already know?"

"What are you saying?" Justin asked, confused.

"Money is the root of all evil, Jack. Since we were younger, we did anything we could to get our hands on it. In order not to slip, you have to learn how to slide."

Justin's face spaced out upon hearing the words spill from Shaun's lips.

"Slick," he mumbled just above a whisper.

"Can you please release my children?" Shaun asked, looking around at the crowd starting to spill out of the church.

"Let them go, Phil," Justin spoke, still locking eyes with Shaun.

When Phil released the kids from his grasp, they ran towards their father, locking on to his legs. Sugar grabbed both of their hands and began to quickly move the opposite way.

"I'm sorry, Shaun. We're just trying to find Reeses. You know she's all we got left."

Shaun thought hard before he spoke. "Marquise Place apartments."

Nodding their heads, Justin and Phil turned around to walk off.

"Jack?" Shaun called out.

Turning around, Justin looked directly into his eyes again. "Yeah?"

"When we meet again, can we please finish our business?" he asked with a taste for blood pumping through his pupils.

"Respect!" Justin agreed.

It was very clear and understood that they next time they crossed paths, somebody wasn't going to make it home to their loved ones.

CHRIS GREEN

Chapter 20

Beno grabbed a towel, covering Reeses as she stood out of the tub. The dark black whip marks on her back were still visible from the vicious beating she took.

"Baby, are you sure you're okay?" Beno asked with concern as he led her back into the bedroom.

"No," she replied with her head down.

"Is there anything I can do to help you feel better?"

Lifting her head, she kissed his lips and slid her tongue into his mouth. Beno closed his eyes, enjoying the taste of her delicate kiss. Unbuckling his pants, he grabbed her wrist in a soft manner.

"Baby, I really think you need some rest. You've been through a lot and I need to talk to you about something," Beno said with a caring voice.

"After," she whispered, letting her towel drop to the floor.

Pushing him lightly down on the bed, she removed his pants, exposing his rock hard manhood. Grabbing his shaft, she used her tongue, licking from the bottom to the top of his rod. She slowly took him deep into her mouth, making her tongue swirl around the head of the monster she controlled.

Beno bit his bottom lip, watching Reeses put her head game down. Her mouth soaked him completely. Chills ran down his spine as he felt the blissful sensation shoot through his stomach.

"Damn, baby!" he grunted, holding the back of her head, gently guiding the rotation of her mouth.

After she assured that his soldier was standing at full attention, she slowly crawled on top of him, running her tongue from his chest up to his neck.

"I love you," she moaned, feeling him slip into her warm kitty.

"I love you too," he whispered, holding her waist tightly.

Rotating her hips, she moved her juice box slowly against his dick, feeling him deep inside her walls. Beno pulled her close to him, smelling the cinnamon scented bath wash pour out of her skin. His lips found her right nipple, sucking it slowly as he moved his hands down to her plump brown apple bottom.

"Oh my God, daddy. I feel it!" Reeses moaned, sliding to the top of his shaft.

Picking her up, Beno flipped her over on all fours, slapping her ass. Positioning himself in between her slit, he rubbed his dick up and down before he entered her slowly.

Reeses leaned forward from his length stretching inside her tight walls. "Baby, please," she whined, grasping the bedsheets tightly.

Beno began to move back and forth slowly, watching her cream on the tip of his manhood. Her Georgia peach jiggled freely as the first orgasm exploded down her leg.

"Oh fuck!" she mumbled with her eyes rolling back inside her head.

Beno couldn't control himself. Her hypnotizing body polluted his brain. Her jet-black hair stretched down her back, laying gently against the crease of her spine.

"Fuck me, daddy," she moaned, tooting her pussy higher in the air for better access.

Beno zoned out, clutching the top of her ass cheeks, sliding deeply in her. Their rhythm began to match and her ass clapped gently against his pelvis while she looked back into his eyes. Feeling his climax coming quickly, he eased out of her warm slit and began to peck her lips slowly down to her belly button. Spreading her legs, he buried his head between her legs. His tongue slid across her clit, licking her sweet juices from her body.

"Shittt!" Reeses gasped, feeling her energy drain from her body.

After finishing his duties, Beno climbed next to her, wrapping his arms tightly around her body. Things were officially back to where they were supposed to be. His love and heart could finally rest.

***

Marquise Place apartments

Justin and Phil made their way quickly up the small flight of steps. Just to be on point, Phil pulled his gun out, clicking off his safety. Stepping in front of apartment A9, Justin knocked on the door twice and stepped back, waiting patiently for an answer.

Phil looked from side to side, making sure nosy neighbors wouldn't be their downfall in case something had to happen in the blink of an eye.

Justin started to knock again, but gripped his gun after hearing the locks unlatch. A red woman opened the door and stared at them with a confused expression.

"Umm, can I help you guys?" she asked with her body hidden behind the door frame.

Phil looked at Justin and back at the woman, who stood in front of them.

"Yeah, we happen to be looking for Slick. Is this his apartment?" Justin asked, hiding his gun behind his back.

"Umm, may I ask who you guys are, and why are you looking for Slick?" she asked with a suspicious expression.

No one knew where she and Slick laid their heads. There were so many enemies in the street who plotted on him. She knew at any time something could easily fall upon them. Her man wasn't going for anything of that nature and she knew he kept their personal life a secret to the outside world.

"My name is Justin, and this is my twin brother. Slick is our uncle," he replied with a huge smile.

Blowing out a huge breath of air, she smiled, stepping from behind the door.

"Oh my God. You're the twins he used to talk about a long time ago. I thought you guys had a prison bid," she replied, shaking Justin's right hand.

"Yeah, we did. We recently got out and wanted to come surprise our uncle personally."

"Oh God. I know he would be happy as hell to see you guys. He stepped out a few hours ago. He might not be back until later tonight. Would you boys like something to drink? You both can keep me company until he comes back."

"Sure," Phil replied quickly with a devilish smile.

"Come in," she said, stepping out of their way. "Lock the door behind you, please." Her iPhone began to ring loudly in her pocket, making her stop in place. "Speaking of the devil." She smiled, picking up the phone.

Phil and Justin eyed her as Slick's voice rang through the phone.

"Baby, guess who's here at the house for you?" she said in an excited tone.

"What? Who's in my house, Natalie? What are you talking 'bout?" Slick asked in a strange voice.

"Your nephews. The twins. They just got out and they're here."

"Natalie, run!" he screamed through the receiver.

Before she could move, Phil aimed his gun at her head, sending her brains flying on the wall behind her.

The phone in her hand bounced across the floor, landing by the couch.

"Natalie! Natalie! What's going on, baby? Talk to me," Slick screamed, breathing erratically.

Phil slowly walked over to the phone, picking it up off the floor. Wiping the blood from the screen, he placed it on speaker phone.

"Long time no see, Unc. Now that I've splatted ya little bitch's brains out, can you please tell us where in the fuck our sister is? The cat and mouse game is over."

"I'm gonna murder you punk-ass street niggas. That's word, on my bitch's life. You will never find that bitch until I get my check, and when you do find her, the bitch's body is gonna be in ten pieces!" Slick screamed loudly through the phone.

"I knew it was you the whole time. Only snake-ass niggas can move they slime ass the way you do. Nothing can be put on your girl's life, pussy, 'cause she's too busy resting in a puddle of brains," Phil said smoothly, as if nothing was wrong.

Snatching the phone from his hands, Justin gritted on his teeth before he spoke. "I swear, if you hurt my fucking sister, you will have to spend the rest of your life hiding under a fucking bridge in France, bitch nigga."

"Justin, mark my words, I'm gonna murder you bitch ass niggas the same way I did your daddy and mama. Be sure of that," Slick added before ending the call.

Justin covered his mouth with pain in his eyes, looking over at Phil. The words that came from Slick's mouth were the beginning to a new war.

"I promise, we gonna kill that snake-ass nigga. We gotta get the fuck outta here. Now!" Phil stated seriously.

Feeling his phone vibrate, Justin pulled out his touch screen, staring at the message on the front of his screen. His eyes grew big and he looked back up at his twin.

"He found her! The little nigga found her," he whispered quickly, rushing out of the door with Phil on his heels.

"Who found her?" Phil asked, clueless, trying to keep up with his brother.

"Beno! The young nigga found her," Justin replied as they jumped in the car and sped off.

Chapter 21

Pulling in front of Beno's house, the twins jumped out, heading towards the front of his porch. Before they could knock, Beno pulled the door open, allowing them to enter. Justin's eyes looked around until his eyes fell on Reeses stepping around the corner.

"Rinesha?" His eyes welled up as he looked at his beautiful sister.

Reeses ran to him. She jumped into his arms, locking on to his neck.

"Alhamdulillah," he mumbled, holding her tightly as if he would lose her.

Dropping tears on his shoulder, Reeses climbed down, making her way to Phil and embracing him with a huge hug.

"It's good to see you too, Reeses," he said in a dry tone.

Releasing him, she looked at them both with tears of joy spilling from her eyes. "When did you all come home? I thought you weren't getting out until December." She wept, staring into Justin's eyes.

"Our lawyer pulled a few strings for us and made it happen a little early. We're just glad you are okay."

"Justin, Slick is - "

"We already know, sis. He's gonna get handled. I promise you on my life he will pay for what he has done," he said sincerely, touching her cheek.

Making her way to Beno, Reeses grabbed his hand, pulling him to her. "I want you both to meet my one and only best friend. This is Beno. I wouldn't be standing here in front of y'all if it wasn't for him," she stated proudly with him hugging her waistline.

"We've already met. I knew that he was a good man when I laid eyes on him," Justin replied, nodding his head to Beno.

Reeses looked at Phil as he eyed Beno with a hint of hatred in his face. Walking over to him, she grabbed his hand, pulling him closer to the three of them.

"I know that I wasn't able to reach you as much when you were doing your bid, but I have something that I have to ask you all," Reeses voiced, looking at the three closest men in her life.

"What is it, baby? Is something wrong?" Beno asked with a hint of curiosity.

"I'll be back," she said, walking off and exiting out the back door of Beno's house.

Beno stared at the twins in confusion, shrugging his shoulders.

Reeses made her way back into the back door with the rolling suitcase in her hand.

"What, are we taking a vacation or something?" Beno asked.

"No."

Taking a deep breath, she spoke the words that were badly eating at her mind. "Since I was younger, I knew I would find my place in something I was truly great at. The shit that I've been through only showed me that there is more in this world than the small things that are given. I'm the daughter of a real savage and I'm ready to take my place for my new life."

"Sis, what are you talking about?" Justin asked, wondering what was up her sleeve.

Opening the suitcase, Reeses flipped the bag, pouring out the huge bundles of blue hundreds. Justin, Phil, and Beno stared in amazement as she looked at them all silently.

"What the fuck?" Phil blurted out, picking up a wad of cash.

"I want this city to be mines. This is two million dollars. Within the next few months, I want the entire city flooded with our product. I'm ready to show these people exactly what the Rivers family is really about. I need all of you guys help to do it."

Grabbing her face, Beno kissed her gently and looked into her beautiful face. "I'm with you on whatever you want to do, my queen, period."

"Hell yeah, I'm in!" Phil smiled, anticipating the new life that was ahead of him.

Nodding her head, Reeses stared at Justin, waiting for his approval.

"Are you sure this is what you want?" he asked with worry in his eyes.

"I'm positive."

"Then you know I'm right here by your side. Just tell me what you want to do, and it's done," Justin replied with a small smile.

"First, I want the biggest ticket placed on Slick's head. A hundred grand for the first person who can deliver him to us. Second, I want the entire city of Atlanta and Smyrna to be ours," she said with confidence.

"Wait, how in the fuck is any of this gonna go down with no dope and no plug?" Phil questioned.

Reeses flashed a big smile from ear to ear. "I already have someone in mind."

Chapter 22

Detective Berkley adjusted his tie before he knocked on Beno's front door. Holding the files in his hand, he looked up as the door came open.

Reeses stood in front of him in Beno's T-shirt with her hair pulled back in a ponytail. "May I help you?" she asked, looking at the white man with a frown.

"Ms. Rivers?" Berkley asked in a shocked tone.

"Yes, who are you?"

"My name is Detective Berkley. I'm the one who's investigating your missing person case. We've been looking everywhere for you, night and day. Is there something I'm missing?" he asked, scratching the top of his head.

"Missing? I've never been missing, sir. It must just be a big misunderstanding," she stated nervously.

"Can you explain the reason your house was a mad wreck? Your friend here seemed to be really worried about you. Don't you think if he filed a missing person report it would be smart to contact the authorities and tell them that you were safe?"

"Sir, no disrespect, but I've had a lot of personal issues going on. I exploded a little and trashed my place. My head was in a lot of different places and I had to leave so I could get a little peace. I would appreciate it if you would leave my personal issues between me and my personal counselor," Reeses said, trying to tighten up her lie quickly.

The detective looked at her with a raised eyebrow, tapping the file in his hand. "What happened to your face and neck?" he asked, gazing at the dark bruises on her.

"To be honest, it's none of your business, Detective. Should I tell you about the razors that I use to slice my legs from time to time? Or what about the lit cigarettes I use to put out on my stomach to ease my depression? Do I have to fill you in on that too?" she asked with a hint of embarrassment.

"No, you don't, ma'am. I came by to talk with Mr. Kelsey about the situation regarding you, but I guess there is no reason for that. Does he happen to be home at this time?"

"Uh, no sir. He stepped out a while earlier. I'm not sure when he will be back."

"The blue Challenger sitting right there belongs to him. Am I correct?"

"Yes, it does. You're saying this because…?" she asked sarcastically.

"Well, Ms. Rivers, since you've been missing, our murder rate has shot through the roof for some odd reason. To make it even stranger, we've gotten over six Crimestopper calls stating they saw a blue Hellcat Challenger leaving two different scenes where a few murders took place."

"Do you know how many Hellcat Challengers you have in this city?"

"A lot, but you don't have too many with twenty-two inch Forgiato rims," the detective stated, waiting for a reply.

Feeling she was about to say the wrong thing, Reeses chose to keep her words to herself.

Clearing his throat, Berkley pulled out his card and handed it to her. "I have a few questions I need to ask him. I'm also investigating the murder of your former boss, Keith Henderson. Do me a favor. Don't leave town anytime soon," he stated with a serious expression, walking off.

Reeses watched him until he climbed in his black Tahoe and pulled off. Closing the door, she quickly made her way to the bedroom waking Beno out of his sleep.

"Beno!" she yelled, shaking his arm.

Jumping up quickly, he hopped out of the bed. "Are you okay? What's wrong?"

"What have you done? A detective just left from the front door saying he needs to talk to you about a murder," she said in a worried tone.

Beno rubbed his hands through his hair, shaking off his sleepiness. "Shit! What did he say?"

"He only said he needs to ask you a few questions."

Snatching some clothes out of his closet, Beno quickly began to put them on. "Get dressed. We have to get away from here. If he wants to ask questions, he obviously don't have anything against me. I bought a house out in Doraville about a week ago. After we get settled, I will get me a lawyer and handle this shit."

Shaking her head, Reeses began to grab all their money, valuables, and important documents. After getting dressed, she made her way across the street to her home, retrieving a few things before they pulled off, leaving Smyrna in their rearview mirror.

Chapter 23
Three months later

Pulling inside the abandoned warehouse, Reeses parked her 2018 Porsche Turbo Machan next to an all-black Cadillac Escalade. Her black Givenchy heels touched the ground as she stepped out of the car, removing her Chanel shades from her face.

"Is this the place?" she asked, looking at Justin getting out of the passenger seat.

"Yes, sis. This is it. They're already waiting inside for us," he said, leading the way.

Her heels clicked across the concrete as she made her way to the entrance of the warehouse. Her hair was wrapped into a bun and her Row Maddly straight leg jeans hugged her juicy bottom comfortably. Her skin boomed with the hint of sweet cinnamon and the little makeup she wore brought out her dark grey eyes.

Walking through the door of the warehouse, Justin led her down a slim hallway. Making a right turn, they climbed a small flight of steps to the next floor. Getting to the top, she spotted Phil standing next to a man who was chained up and dangling from the ceiling.

"I told you the nigga wasn't dead," Phil smirked, stepping back.

Giving Phil a dismissive look, Reeses grabbed the black bag, snatching it from the top of his head.

Quay breathed harshly, staring Reeses in her eyes. The huge scars that covered the top of his body flashed her mind back to the day she had shaved her blade inside his neck.

"I watched you die. It's impossible," she said, staring into his eyes.

"A lot of things are impossible. It doesn't matter what you do to me, bitch! You're still gonna die."

Reeses smiled, touching the side of his face, shaking her head. "Justin, can you please make your sister feel better?"

Stepping in front of him, Justin pulled his 44 Magnum bulldog from his hip. "Where is Slick?" he asked humbly.

"You're wasting your time, busta-ass nigga!"

The gun roared, knocking half of Quay's head to the floor.

"The same thing goes. I want more men in the streets looking for this bum. Night and day, nobody is to rest until that son of a bitch is inside of a grave. Can you please get rid of him for me?" she said, looking at Justin, putting her glasses back on.

"Right away, sis," he said, jumping into action.

"Phil, I need you to follow me out to the house. Beno has the next shipment ready to drop off on the west. Don't worry about picking up the money. I will send Beno to handle it later today," she said, walking off.

Phil mugged her on the sly as they made their way outside towards the cars.

***

Pulling into the driveway of a large home, Reeses parked her car next to Beno's Challenger. Phil pulled in directly behind her in his 2017 Buick Verano.

Heading inside, they walked into the kitchen, where Beno sat counting up the large bills that filled up the kitchen table. Kissing him on the cheek and lips, Reeses took a seat across from him while Phil posted against the Subzero refrigerator.

"Is everything okay?" he asked, looking at her for a slight moment.

"He's gone," she replied, as if everything was normal with having another person murdered for the price of disrespect.

"Have you heard anything else about that slimeball?" he asked, referring to Slick.

"No, but I've put everyone at the spot on point. I want him dead and I'm not gonna stop until he pays for what he has done to this family."

"I understand."

"Uh, I don't mean to break up you guys' little conversation, but it's three o'clock and I still got my own shit to handle. So can we bag this shit up and get it on the road, please?" Phil asked in an aggravated tone.

Beno set down the money, looking at him with hate written over his face. The past three months had been rough dealing with him. One minute would be cool then the next would be pure hell around him. In his eyes, the only one who seemed to have any sense was Justin.

"Are you straight, my nigga? Why do you always gotta bring that negative ass energy over to my crib?" Beno asked restarting his count.

"First of all, nigga, this my sister shit. You only fucking her, li'l bruh! You ain't the one who putting the bread in my pocket. So if you can just bag that shit up, I can put in the real work and get this shit handled."

"Hey, we're not about to start this shit! You two do this shit every time you're around each other. Can we please keep our mind focused on the business?" Reeses spat, getting tired of the feud they held inside for whatever reason.

"Nah, fuck that! Who do the fuck you think you are? This is my home and I wouldn't give a damn if she was your sister or not. She's my girl and soon to be my wife. You don't run shit. We brought you into this business with us, something that you don't have to be a part of. You can walk out anytime, and our money is still gonna be made without you or your negative-ass attitude, my guy," Beno replied, pointing down at the table.

Reeses slid her fingers through her hair, knowing where the conversation was about to lead to.

Laughing loudly, Phil took a deep breath. "Bro, what makes you think that all of this is yours? Huh? The same way you got this shit, you can lose it, my nigga. Let me explain a little bit better. When you were going to middle school with my sister, walking around getting bitched out by niggas you got to go to school with, I was running around putting that smoke pole on bustas like yo' daddy. I make it my business to wake up and get to this paper. So this is part of my shit too. You think just 'cause you kill a few niggas that shit bump yo' status up from being a nobody? And for the record, I don't like you. My reason why is this family is built of loyalty. We all have our slips, but this shit runs through our blood. You don't even fit the description. You gotta prove yourself to this family before anybody can trust you, nigga. We don't get comfortable with just anyone and prison changed a lot of shit, my boy."

"Reeses, can I see you in the other room? Now!" Beno demanded, stepping away from the table.

Taking a deep breath, Reeses shot daggers into Phil's eyes before she made her way into the living room. She could tell from the expression on Beno's face that he was about to snap into his feelings.

"I'm starting not to be sure about this anymore, Reese. Your brother is out of control and I don't think he needs to be part of this."

"Beno, I've told you time after time, Phil is only trying to get under your skin. We're supposed to be making money and y'all running around here beefing like two petty kids. He's my brother, for Christ sake," Reeses stressed with an exhausted face.

"Well, your fucking brother needs to learn some respect. How can we focus on getting money if we got this bad energy-ass nigga around? I'm starting to feel he wants the position you're in but is shooting at me to take it. The nigga is slime and I don't like him!"

"Well, guess what? I'll be the one making the decision on that matter. My brothers need my help and I'm gonna be the brain for it. Focus on the money, bae, and let me handle the rest," Reeses stated with confidence.

Containing his anger, Beno smiled, shaking his head in a disappointed manner. "Seems like you don't know what you doing," he mocked before heading upstairs.

After watching him disappear to the second floor of the house, Reeses made her way back into the kitchen.

"Why do you always insist on coming over here to upset shit, Phil? That shit isn't cool. If we're gonna make money, I'm with it, but if this little beef you two are holding on your chest keeps going, I'm gonna just handle this on my own," Reeses said, taking a seat at the table.

"It's starting to seem like this nigga comes before family. Don't get this shit confused, li'l sis. I'm in this shit for the paper. Either you want me to handle the job or not."

***

After dumping the weight off at the last two spots, Phil waited patiently for the worker to come back up front with the cash re-up. He began to grow impatient, but rose to his feet after seeing him return from the back.

"You got that ready or what?" Phil asked, looking at his empty hands.

"I was told to hold on to it, Phil. Justin will be through here later to pick it up from me."

"Wait a minute! What?"

"Reeses called and told me to hold the profit until Justin pulls up. I'm just following orders, bro," the man replied, shrugging his shoulders.

It was now clear to Phil the message that Reeses was sending. She was trying to cut him out of the entire motion. His anger started to boil over as he thought about his kiss ass brother, who cherished every step she took.

Pulling his gun, Phil squeezed his trigger, sending a bullet through the back of the man's head. His soulless body fell against the couch and slumped down to the floor. Phil moved quickly through the hallway, scanning each room. He slowed his pace after spotting the black suitcase lying next to a bedroom wall.

Snatching it up, he moved to the front door and left as quickly as he came.

***

It was around ten a.m. when Phil pulled inside his ducked off apartment complex. Shutting off his car, he reached in the back, grabbing the case. Hearing his phone vibrate, he chose to ignore it as he climbed out of the vehicle, heading for his door.

"Do you mind if I holla at you for a minute?" Phil heard the voice speak before he could take another step.

Jolting his body around quickly, he grabbed the handle of his gun, facing Slick, who sat inside the front seat of a black Chrysler 300.

"Hold up! I just want to talk. I didn't come for any problems," Slick said, holding his hands above the window so Phil could see them.

"You pussy-ass nigga! You got a lot of nerve sliding up on me screaming you wanna talk after that promise you made over the phone. Do you know the type of price that's on your head right now?" Phil replied, itching to pull his burner.

"I know the family is not seeing eye to eye right now and a lot of different stories are going around about what's going on. I pulled up on you because you've always been the easy nephew who can understand and listen a little more. Justin is always gonna be rebellious. That's why I came to speak with you," he lied, firing up the menthol cigarette.

"You talking right now and so far, I ain't heard shit that's calming my actions on blowing yo' stupid ass away. What the fuck do you want?"

"I want peace, and I want to get you rich. You smarter that ya brother and sister, Phil. You'd rather be a drop off man instead of making yo' own millions? You a leader, nephew, but as long as you sit back and get used, you will never get anywhere. Just take a ride with me. If you ain't interested by the time I'm done talking, then you can just kill me and be done with it."

Phil held eye contact, evaluating his uncle's words. Looking down at the case full of money, a brilliant idea flashed before his eyes.

"If this shit ain't 'bout no real paper, we gon' handle our business exactly where we stand," Phil replied with a serious expression, jumping in the passenger seat.

"Paper is all I know, nephew," Slick said with an evil smile as he rolled up the windows to the tinted black Chrysler and pulled off.

To Be Continued…
True Savage 5
Coming Soon

Submission Guideline.

Submit the first three chapters of your completed manuscript to ldpsubmissions@gmail.com, subject line: Your book's title. The manuscript must be in a .doc file and sent as an attachment. Document should be in Times New Roman, double spaced and in size 12 font. Also, provide your synopsis and full contact information. If sending multiple submissions, they must each be in a separate email.

Have a story but no way to send it electronically? You can still submit to LDP/Ca$h Presents. Send in the first three chapters, written or typed, of your completed manuscript to:

LDP: Submissions Dept
Po Box 870494
Mesquite, Tx 75187

DO NOT send original manuscript. Must be a duplicate.

Provide your synopsis and a cover letter containing your full contact information.

Thanks for considering LDP and Ca$h Presents.

CHRIS GREEN

Coming Soon from Lock Down Publications/Ca$h Presents

BOW DOWN TO MY GANGSTA
By **Ca$h**
TORN BETWEEN TWO
By **Coffee**
BLOOD STAINS OF A SHOTTA **III**
By **Jamaica**
WHEN THE STREETS CLAP BACK **III**
By **Jibril Williams**
STEADY MOBBIN
By **Marcellus Allen**
BLOOD OF A BOSS **V**
By **Askari**
LOYAL TO THE GAME **IV**
By **T.J. & Jelissa**
A DOPEBOY'S PRAYER **II**
By **Eddie "Wolf" Lee**
IF LOVING YOU IS WRONG… **III**
LOVE ME EVEN WHEN IT HURTS
By **Jelissa**
DAUGHTERS OF A SAVAGE **II**
By **Chris Green**
TRAPHOUSE KING **II**
By **Hood Rich**
BLAST FOR ME **II**
RAISED AS A GOON **V**

188

By **Ghost**

ADDICTIED TO THE DRAMA **III**

By **Jamila Mathis**

LIPSTICK KILLAH **III**

By **Mimi**

WHAT BAD BITCHES DO **II**

By **Aryanna**

THE COST OF LOYALTY **II**

By **Kweli**

SHE FELL IN LOVE WITH A REAL ONE

By **Tamara Butler**

LOVE SHOULDN'T HURT

By **Meesha**

CORRUPTED BY A GANGSTA **II**

By **Destiny Skai**

SHE FELL IN LOVE WITH A REAL ONE II

By **Tamara Butler**

Available Now

RESTRAINING ORDER **I & II**

By **CA$H & Coffee**

LOVE KNOWS NO BOUNDARIES **I II & III**

By **Coffee**

RAISED AS A GOON I, II, III & IV

BRED BY THE SLUMS I, II, III

BLAST FOR ME

By **Ghost**

LAY IT DOWN **I & II**

LAST OF A DYING BREED

BLOOD STAINS OF A SHOTTA I & II

By **Jamaica**

LOYAL TO THE GAME

LOYAL TO THE GAME II

LOYAL TO THE GAME III

By **TJ & Jelissa**

BLOODY COMMAS I & II

SKI MASK CARTEL I & II

By **T.J. Edwards**

IF LOVING HIM IS WRONG...I & II

By **Jelissa**

WHEN THE STREETS CLAP BACK I & II

By **Jibril Williams**

A DISTINGUISHED THUG STOLE MY HEART I II & III

By **Meesha**

PUSH IT TO THE LIMIT

By **Bre' Hayes**

BLOOD OF A BOSS **I, II, III & IV**

By **Askari**

THE STREETS BLEED MURDER **I, II & III**

THE HEART OF A GANGSTA I II& III

By **Jerry Jackson**

CUM FOR ME

CUM FOR ME 2

CUM FOR ME 3

An **LDP Erotica Collaboration**

BRIDE OF A HUSTLA **I II & II**

THE FETTI GIRLS **I, II& III**

CORRUPTED BY A GANGSTA

By **Destiny Skai**

WHEN A GOOD GIRL GOES BAD

By **Adrienne**

A GANGSTER'S REVENGE **I II III & IV**

THE BOSS MAN'S DAUGHTERS

THE BOSS MAN'S DAUGHTERS II

THE BOSSMAN'S DAUGHTERS III

THE BOSSMAN'S DAUGHTERS IV

A SAVAGE LOVE **I & II**

BAE BELONGS TO ME

A HUSTLER'S DECEIT I, II

By **Aryanna**

A KINGPIN'S AMBITON

A KINGPIN'S AMBITION **II**

I MURDER FOR THE DOUGH

By **Ambitious**

TRUE SAVAGE

TRUE SAVAGE II

TRUE SAVAGE **III**

TRUE SAVAGE **IV**

By **Chris Green**

A DOPEBOY'S PRAYER

By **Eddie "Wolf" Lee**

THE KING CARTEL **I, II & III**

By **Frank Gresham**

THESE NIGGAS AIN'T LOYAL **I, II & III**

By **Nikki Tee**

GANGSTA SHYT **I II &III**

By **CATO**

THE ULTIMATE BETRAYAL

By **Phoenix**

BOSS'N UP **I , II & III**

By **Royal Nicole**

I LOVE YOU TO DEATH

By Destiny J

I RIDE FOR MY HITTA

I STILL RIDE FOR MY HITTA

By **Misty Holt**

LOVE & CHASIN' PAPER

By **Qay Crockett**

TO DIE IN VAIN

By **ASAD**

BROOKLYN HUSTLAZ

By **Boogsy Morina**

BROOKLYN ON LOCK I & II

By **Sonovia**

GANGSTA CITY

By **Teddy Duke**

A DRUG KING AND HIS DIAMOND I & II

A DOPEMAN'S RICHES

By Nicole Goosby

<u>TRAPHOUSE KING</u>

By **Hood Rich**

<u>LIPSTICK KILLAH **I, II**</u>

By **Mimi**

BOOKS BY LDP'S CEO, CA$H

TRUST IN NO MAN

TRUST IN NO MAN 2

TRUST IN NO MAN 3

BONDED BY BLOOD

SHORTY GOT A THUG

THUGS CRY

THUGS CRY 2

THUGS CRY 3

TRUST NO BITCH

TRUST NO BITCH 2

TRUST NO BITCH 3

TIL MY CASKET DROPS

RESTRAINING ORDER

RESTRAINING ORDER 2

IN LOVE WITH A CONVICT

Coming Soon

BONDED BY BLOOD 2

BOW DOWN TO MY GANGSTA